'"I say we can manage n ... than you, Terry. OK, so a fiver's not much, ... further than a bloke ca...

There was silence. I shi... was too busy smiling i... point and made it well... a convincing argume... the boy she loved. But I knew ... that magnetic quality that attracted you to things you've begun to distrust, all gave me a terrifying insight into what was going to happen next. It was going to be something I couldn't handle, and Terry would offer it, and I wouldn't be able to refuse.

"Betcha!" Terry said, quietly, evenly.'

The bet was crazy from the start. There was no way anyone could get from Liverpool to Scotland on only five pounds – especially with fun-loving Bel in tow. But Megan couldn't lose this chance to prove herself to sarky Terry Macdolan. He'd been getting at her ever since he paired up with Bel, her best friend, and now Megan was tired of playing the jealous gooseberry.

But the trip was to be far more surprising than even Megan could have imagined. For Michael O'Connor, an American student, was also on the road, and he would lead Megan into a momentous adventure . . .

Another novel by Barbara Jacobs, STICK, is also available in Corgi Freeway.

JUST HOW FAR?

BARBARA JACOBS

with best wishes
Barbara Jacobs

CORGI
F·R·E·E·W·A·Y

JUST HOW FAR?

A CORGI FREEWAY BOOK 0 552 524743

Originally published in Great Britain by
Corgi Freeway Books

PRINTING HISTORY

Corgi Freeway edition published 1989

This book is set in 11/12 pt Palatino
by Colset Private Limited, Singapore.

Corgi Freeway Books are published by Transworld Publishers Ltd., 61–63 Uxbridge Road, Ealing, London W5 5SA, in Australia by Transworld Publishers (Australia) Pty. Ltd., 15–23 Helles Avenue, Moorebank, NSW 2170, and in New Zealand by Transworld Publishers (N.Z.) Ltd., Cnr. Moselle and Waipareira Avenues, Henderson, Auckland.

Made and printed in Great Britain by
Cox & Wyman Ltd., Reading, Berks.

JUST HOW FAR?

Chapter One

The first time you fall in love is very different from the first time you feel love. At least, that's what I've discovered. Feelings aren't to be completely trusted, they possess you like devils. Only a few weeks ago I was possessed, mind, heart and soul, by a devil called Terry Macdolan.

I met him at a party; one of those riots in a darkened house with empty lager cans littering the stairs and reggae music cracking the windows, that pass for parties in Liverpool. That time, I'd gone alone because Bel was at a wedding party given by one of her cousins in Bootle. It was Saturday night and I'd washed my hair on Friday, so there was no excuse to sit at home watching my mum and dad setting the world to rights and sorting out other people's problems.

Terry Macdolan was in the kitchen at the party, under the table, barking at the cat.

'Who're you?' I asked.

'St Bernard,' he said. 'Who're you?'

'Megan Griffiths,' I told him. That was my problem, not being able to come up with anything more interesting than the truth. It's a major failing in a Merseysider.

I lured him from under the table with an unopened can of lager I'd found in the twin-tub, but I often, afterwards, wished I hadn't. Until then, all the boys I'd met had been spotty friends, seriously intense about chess, politics and pop music. Terry Macdolan was casual, off-hand, as laid-back as a piranha fish, and beautiful. Right, that's weird, describing a boy as beautiful, and normally I'd be the last person in the world to indulge in such flights of heart-pounding fancy, but as I said, I felt love for the first time and the feelings got in the way of factual appraisal. He had coffee-coloured skin, upturned brown eyes, and a similarly upturned grin in one corner of his mouth. He also had a gap between his front teeth. Why that should have struck me as being beautiful, I didn't know then, and I still don't know, although my ideas of beauty have changed since. All I knew was that the combination of coffee and cream, gaps and slants, had the effect of drying out my throat and kicking in both my knees at the same time.

We talked, until someone shouted, 'Police!' But as he ran, he grabbed my hand. He walked me home. I suppose you could say that he talked me home, and added to my sore throat and knee injuries by seducing me with a non-stop stream of jokes, anecdotes and carefully edited portions of his life history which were as sad as they were funny.

He was fascinating, charming and relentlessly attractive; intelligent and witty and lazy enough for me to tell him that I could help to reform him and retrieve the potential for success that surely had to be there, despite his months of unemployment and his amusingly cynical view of life. Mentally, I wrote a scenario in which he would fall hopelessly in love with me, and, with the support of my own helpless love, would rise to great things in life: a university graduate, an actor, a businessman.

Now I know that he must have sensed this dreadful need in me to reform and reshape him, and backed away from it. Terry didn't want to be saved. Then, I only noticed that he didn't seem as keen as I was for the statutory five minutes or more of good-night kisses, and that my desperate question, 'When will I see you again?' led only to a rather off-hand, 'I'll be around. I'll find you. You might catch me at . . .' and he reeled off the names of several cellar bars and the names of people I'd never heard of. Then, finally, he flashed his incredible smile at me, and disappeared. I couldn't stop thinking about that smile.

For days afterwards I reconstructed the conversation I'd had with him. I remembered only his brilliance, his sarcastically attractive wit, and his eyes. I had to find him again. So, as soon as Bel and I had saved up a pound between us, I started to drag her round the cellars, looking for him.

I didn't say that we were actually looking for him. I didn't mention him, except in that fairly throw-away style which he'd taught me, briefly. I didn't say that he'd taken my mind completely off my exam results, nor that he was the most exciting thing that had happened to me since the day I was delivered in the ambulance going to hospital, which was hearsay excitement and imagining, not the real thing. Goodness knows why I kept the feeling from Bel. Sharing it, at that early stage, just a brief confession, 'I've met this Terry, and I can't breathe for thinking about him,' would have saved me from the subsequent agony. But there you go. All mistakes have 'if only . . .' endings.

On the third night of cellar-hopping, we found him. And Terry fell for my best friend, Bel. She's as exotic as I'm freckly Welsh-Liverpudlian. She's skinny and foxy, Barbadian two generations back, funny, clever going on stupid, and as wild as I'm practical.

'There, that's the bloke I met at the party,' I told her

when we'd completed a whole circuit of the catacombed cellar, and she said, 'Oh him? Yeah, I've met his type before.' I suppose that was Bel's way of falling in love. Terry spent the whole evening talking at me and grinning lopsidedly at Bel. Afterwards she said, 'Terry wants us to go out with him next Thursday. He'll make Benno come along for you.' There's no arguing with Bel when she's in that sort of mood, no point in saying, 'Benno would be more comfortable on four legs than two, and I don't like his scratchy pink skin, or his snout,' because I knew she hadn't noticed that Terry's friend, Benno, was a pig. She hadn't noticed anything except Terry.

From that moment on, it was Terry and Bel, Bel and Terry, and Megan gooseberry, almost every night of July. The summer holidays were slipping away in darkness. I'm not just talking here about that cellar, either. I'm talking about feelings, not to be trusted, but totally, depressingly, screamingly consuming, especially when you're keeping them to yourself. Feeling love isn't all it's cracked up to be.

Bel had no idea. Terry, though, knew exactly what was going on in my wildest imaginings. From time to time he'd glance at me with just the right amount of X-ray in his slanting eyes, and he'd accompany that with one of his funny comments, especially geared to getting my back up. Now, because he'd found someone who just liked him for exactly what he was, it gave him the confidence to snipe at me and my do-gooding love that had come to nothing. It was almost as if he were showing off to me by demonstrating his success with Bel. He noticed every one of my vulnerabilities and aimed his darts into the heart of each. He taunted me for my red hair, my exam anxiety, my smug middle-class ways, grinning when I struggled to come back at him with a similar barb.

Bel, in a stupid daze of love, kept saying, 'Why d'you have to get at Terry? I know you don't like him much, but he's not bad if you'd give yourself a chance to get to know him.'

Chance would have been a fine thing.

Terry was unemployed, more out of choice, I always thought, than misfortune. He'd ploughed in his A levels and set himself up as a kind of cellar philosopher, surrounding himself with characters like Benno and Yob, a shrunken kid of about seventeen who worked Saturdays in the market and drew dole money for the rest of week. The three of them made a virtue of poverty, to the extent of begging from Bel and me who were, after all, living on pocket-money. It was always, 'Share your bag of chips, girls?' and 'Clear out your pockets and we'll go five ways for the next lager.'

Bel began to notice it, too. 'God, don't they go on about how skint they are!' she complained to me one night on the way home. Suddenly, I saw light at the end of the tunnel. Female solidarity. The best friend who used to be around was still there, under layers of all-accepting love. Bel always had been accepting, I was the reformer, but this time she and I saw eye to eye on something. I could make something out of that. What I made was another huge mistake, the next Wednesday.

We were all sitting, as usual, round the scuffed table in the furthest reaches of the cellar, and Bel was moaning to anyone who'd listen about wanting to go on a day-trip to Southport.

'Southport?' Terry sneered. 'Might as well ask me to take you on a world cruise. It's train fare, or bus fare, food money, amusements money, all that! Look, Bel, no socks. I got no socks, and you want me to shell out for seasides? How many times do we have to tell you? We're skint. Boracic. Hard up. Down to our last empty tin of shandy and four straws until you buy us another. It's your round, by the way!'

Bel shook her tight curls and turquoise hoop earrings at him. It was the closest I'd ever seen to a small rebellion. I smiled inside.

'Listen to it! Just listen to it!' she shrieked. 'Can't manage on thirty quid a week! Remember when you used to go to school like us, Terry? Thirty quid a week was a fortune, then.'

'He never did go to school. He used to go as far as the bike sheds, decide he'd had enough, and leg it,' I grinned.

'A real education, them bike sheds,' Terry remembered.

'Thirty quid . . . I reckon I could live for a month on thirty quid,' Bel grumbled, shaking her head in wonder.

'Yeah,' I agreed. 'My dad says he can remember the days when you could buy five ciggies in a paper bag, go for a walk on the Pier Head, buy a *Liverpool Echo*, and still have change from a fifty-pound note . . .'

'Be serious for once,' Bel said, nudging me.

But I was serious, in my own way. Seriously happy, for the first time in over a month, about feeling that Bel and I were on the same side, and that Terry was the one taking the strain. His eyes glinted like a ferret's, blood-red in candlelight.

'Right. Be serious. Youse, smart-arse, bet you couldn't live for a week on the dole!' he snarled at me, leaving Bel out of it.

'Serious? Bel and I could live comfortably on a fiver, couldn't we, kiddo?' I snarled back.

'I reckon I could make a fiver last a month,' Bel dreamed. Better and better.

'And go for day-trips to Southport?' Terry asked, sarcastically.

'Further!' I snapped.

Terry's eyes turned to broken glass.

'That's what we all need, eh, Benno? A girl who'll go further on a fiver!'

'Aw, you shut up, you!' Bel shouted at him, linking her arm with mine. My best mate, again. 'It always comes down to the same thing with you lot, doesn't it? I say we can manage money better than you, Terry. OK, so a fiver's not much, but a woman can make it stretch further than a bloke can. Can't we, Meg?'

There was silence. I shivered. Bel didn't seem to notice, she was too busy smiling in empty triumph at having made her point and made it well, and perhaps in having put forward a convincing argument for a day-trip to Southport with the boy she loved. But I knew better. Feelings, intuition, that magnetic quality that attracted you to things you've begun to distrust, all gave me a terrifying insight into what was going to happen next. It was going to be something I couldn't handle, and Terry would offer it, and I wouldn't be able to refuse.

'Betcha!' Terry said, quietly, evenly.

'Huh?' Bel asked.

'So how long do you reckon you could live on a fiver?' he persisted.

'A week at least,' she giggled.

I glanced at both of them, Bel's happy innocence, Terry's smirking, and felt something tighten up and begin to crawl along my spine.

'And you, Miss Tomato Head. You reckon you could get past Southport, do you?' he asked me.

'On a fiver? Try me,' I couldn't help saying.

'Yer on. Betcha. Betcha both. You're just schoolkids. You've never lived where we are. You don't know the half of it. It's cruel, over on our side, and it costs. So I'm making this little bet with you. Right?'

Slowly, he pulled two five-pound notes from his pocket, and handed one to each of us. Bel gulped and goggled at him. I bit my bottom lip.

'There's a fiver each. And each of these says you can't live like a human being. Ask me how I know? Because that's what they whisper to me out of my back pocket every time I pick up the dole. "Terry Macdolan, you're a sub-human, and six of us, each week, are going to prove it!" So you've only got one fiver each. That's my food, and my social life, and my bus fares, and my job application money for forty-eight snivelling hours, right . . .'

'Terry, don't get heavy!' Bel pleaded.

'You started it!' he snapped. 'You know it all, don't you? So there's the money, now prove it! You see how long you can make it last. I say you might just be able to cadge a lift to Southport with it. And if you do, if you make it stretch, let's see . . . as far as Scotland, eh? . . . I'll take you to Southport to celebrate, and we'll all be human beings for a day. Can't say fairer than that!'

'Scotland?' Bel breathed.

'Scotland? Easy!' I heard myself pretending. 'Come on, Bel! Let's prove we can earn ourselves a day at the seaside. We can do it!'

'Can we?' Bel asked, smiling weakly.

' 'Course we can,' I said.

'No chance,' Terry said, at the same time.

Even then I knew that he was right, and that I was wrong. Something you never do with devils is to back them into corners, because the only way they have to escape is to bite you where it hurts. This wasn't anything to do with Bel and Terry, and nothing to do with a day-trip to Southport. It was to do with feelings, about revenge and hurt pride, about winning and losing, about Terry and me.

'We'll go tomorrow,' I said.

'Day after,' Bel said.

'Done, then?' Terry asked.

'Well done,' I admitted.

Chapter Two

Life would be a lot simpler if conversations could run on the lines of:

'Hello. I love you.'

'Sorry. You're out of luck. I fancy your friend.'

'Kind of you to tell me. I'll now remove myself from your hair.'

I had conversations like that, scaled down a little, when I was seven. Everyone knew where they stood, and what order they stood in. But games start taking over, later on, like the game Terry and Bel and I were playing: Trivial Pursuit, maybe? Now, from the smug position of having played that, lost, and survived to play something more worthwhile, I can sneer. Then, I thought I was proving something about myself that might make Terry decide I wasn't something orange-coloured and nasty that had got itself stuck to his boot.

Bel, I knew, was merely confused by the turn the routine evening in the cellar bar had taken. I expected her round at my house the next morning, her bravado eaten away by panic. She has moods. I suppose I do, too, but mine are more brooding. Bel's are quite dramatic.

'No way!' she announced, when I answered her frantic ringing at my doorbell. 'There's just no way I can get round the old man on this one. I've been lying awake all night but I just can't see my way through. Come 'e'd, Meg. You know what my dad is like! Two girls hitching up the M-whatever, one of them his sweet six-year-old daughter? No way!'

She threw her arms and her voice around all the way up our stairs. I'd had demonstrations like this from her before.

'He's going to send me back to Barbados when he finds out,' she howled when I'd settled her into a chair.

'Back? You've never been there. Nor has he. He was born in Bootle,' I reminded her.

'OK, OK, start confusing me with logic! It just won't work. Terry's mad, I'm mad, you're mad. And my dad'll be madder than all of us,' she screamed.

'Look, look at this map. That's where we're going, tomorrow morning. Blackpool, to my Aunty Esme's guest-house . . .'

'Not the place with the polystyrene gravy?' she shuddered.

'Right. The place we went to when we were ten. Your mum and dad were pretty keen for you to come to my Aunty Esme's then, weren't they? So that's the cover-story. You can tell them you'll be staying there with me, for a week or so. Unexpected holiday!' I grinned.

'Too unexpected for my mum. When will she have time to buy out C & A for my holiday outfits?'

I shrugged.

'You'll have to sort that out with her. But my mum and dad know the whole story, and they're quite excited. Mum'll drive us all the way to Blackpool. My dad keeps telling me about his hiking trips. It's pretty encouraging.'

'But . . . if I'm supposed to be going to your Aunt Esme's, how do I pack food to take with us? Terry said we could take all the food we could carry, but I can't persuade my mum that I'll need food in a guest-house.'

'I'll bring the food,' I told her. 'And I'll share your clothes if I run out, OK?'

'Right . . .' she said, dubiously, looking down at her poppy-coloured satin jacket and across at my ginger hair. 'Er . . . right.'

'So Aunty Esme's is the first stop. One night in Blackpool, then on to Scotland,' I smiled, seeing her to the door as she rehearsed, under her breath, 'We're off to Blackpool in the morning, Dad, with Megan's mum. Won't that be fun?' It sounded unconvinced and unconvincing. I left her to it, mumbling her way down the street, and went up to continue the planning, poring over the map, trying to make sense of a route to Scotland that wouldn't cost anything and wouldn't wear Bel's legs away.

Haverigg. I saw the name on the map, leaning off the Cumbrian coast, and swallowed hard. Pete Hanson. That was the boy's name. I'd written to him several times the summer before last, after the brief encounter in Weymouth that had ended with a fumbled kiss outside our caravan. I'd been lovesick and fourteen. We'd exchanged addresses. His parents had smiled indulgently at my parting tears and his embarrassed smiles and murmured, 'Now, any time you come up to the Lakes, do drop in and see us!' as I'd slipped a soppy poem into his sweaty palm. He'd written out his address for me, in capital letters: East Street, Haverigg. The romance had come to nothing. He'd never answered any of the letters, but his face, with that embarrassed smile, had looked up at me from its secret hiding-place under my alarm clock until I spilled Lucozade on my bedside table in a fit of chicken-pox just before the following Christmas. The photo had become too sticky and bitty to kiss after that, and was left to disintegrate in my wastepaper basket with the torn-up letters I hadn't posted.

Still, embarrassment aside, holiday romances could be followed up, if the need arose. The need was arising now. I circled Haverigg on the map, and bit my pencil. Carlisle to Haverigg was a long haul. Perhaps two or three days, depending on lifts and strength, but once in Carlisle we could almost stretch across the Scottish border and then fly back to give the thumbs-up-our-nose to Terry know-all.

Dad offered me a tent, a sleeping-bag, a bobble-hat and a nineteen-sixties' edition of the youth hostels handbook. The tent was one of those you need an army of Boy Scouts to carry for you, and the sleeping-bag had belonged to our dog Ripper until the day he died on it. I refused both, politely. My father's out of touch with me, but tries his best to be interested. My wild bet with Terry had obviously stirred some old memories up. He and Mum spent most of the evening discussing the 'far-out' holiday they'd spent hitching through Europe in 1967. It sounded fab, groovy and gear. They lost me somewhere on the road between Liverpool and Dover and didn't even notice that I'd slipped out to my room to pack.

'Well, it's the Big Day today,' Dad boomed, when I staggered down next morning.

Mum had her tense face and her glasses on. That was because she'd volunteered to drive us to Blackpool and feels even less comfortable as a driver than as a forty year old.

'Bel's father telephoned,' Dad mumbled between mouthfuls of toast. 'He wanted to know the full details of this trip.'

'You didn't tell him?' I stammered.

'What do you think? I told him you were staying with your mum's sister, and that she was a reasonable person, and that if it was humanly possible she'd see that you were in bed at a reasonable hour, and take written statements of intent from any male over the age of eleven who looked at your knees,' Dad said, in his usual dry way.

'You never!'

'No, I never,' he mimicked, cruelly. 'Not the bit about the knees, anyway. But I did say that it was just possible she might take you on a day-trip to the Lake District. That way we cover ourselves, don't we?'

'Can't be too careful with Bel's family,' Mum said.

Dad pulled a face. I suddenly saw the advantages of being their daughter.

'Better get going, then,' I sighed, putting down my piece of toast. Mum and Dad looked at each other. Dad cleared his throat.

'Megan . . .' he said, looking uncomfortable.

'What your father's trying to say . . .' Mum interrrupted.

'No, Dilys. Let me. Now, it's like this,' Dad stammered. 'We've always tried to encourage your independence, haven't we? And we're not going to suggest, at this point in time, that the world is a rather less attractive place than it seems to be, but . . .'

'Don't split up,' Mum said quickly. 'Don't, please don't, hitch-hike on your own. I know you're a level-headed girl, and that you know how to look after yourself, but we'd like you to take that one little precaution. And this.' She pushed a small whistle-thing into my hand. 'It's a screamer. Pull that cord and it screams, see? Times are different now from the way they were in the sixties. Just look after yourself, that's all.'

To my surprise, two reluctant tears wormed down

my cheeks. Some girls get hugs and kisses and cotton-wool insulation jackets, or satin jackets, to protect them from the world. I got a little whistle that screams when rape is imminent, and it seemed a gesture as intimate as a kiss. It made me feel small and vulnerable. I didn't want to go. I was scared.

But Dad hauled my haversack into the car, rattling tins and all, and Mum finally got the engine kicking over. To say, 'Look here, folks, I think I've changed my mind about this,' would have spoiled the unique double-act they'd perfected over the sixteen years of my life, so I just waved politely to Dad and sat clutching my knees and blinking while Mum hunched over the wheel, kangarooing us to Bel's.

Bel was waiting on the pavement outside her house, sitting on what looked like a cabin-trunk. Her mother was standing guard at the front door, arms folded, best purple dress, two rows of pearls.

'Come in! Come in and have a little cup of tea!' she shouted.

Mum refused, carefully, keeping the engine running, trying to explain that if she let the car cool down it might never spring into life again, so the family was called out to launch Bel's case on to the car roof.

'Why're you bringing your fitted wardrobe?' I hissed at Bel as she slid into the back seat.

She groaned.

'Don't!' she mouthed back, then allowed herself to be pulled through the window for noisy kisses.

'You mind your manners now, girl!'

'And be in bed no later than ten-thirty.'

'Bring me a stick of rock, our kid.'

'And one of them hats!'

'I want . . .'

'Shush now, don't cry, Ma. It's only a week!'

Bel's father said, curling his arm round her mother's ample shoulders and trying to detach her from the car window as we pulled away.

Bel remained turned towards the noisy waving group until they were no more than dots in the distance.

'The toe-rag!' she snarled finally, turning in fury, arms folded.

'Who?' I gaped.

'Terry! Him with the mouth. Wouldn't you've thought he'd be there to see us off?'

'No chance,' I grinned.

'You don't like him much, do you, kiddo?' she laughed.

'Not much.'

'Just at this moment,' she sighed, 'me neither.'

Chapter Three

If I was a town, I'd be Blaenau Ffestiniog. If Bel was a town she'd be Blackpool. She looked like a homing parrot on its perch, sitting in Aunty Esme's cluttered dining-room surrounded by plastic portraits of Charles and Di, Andy and Fergie, several children with eyes like aliens, and a Chinese girl with a green face. Our tablemats had pictures of the Houses of Parliament or St Paul's Cathedral on them, and there was tomato sauce in a plastic tomato, brown sauce in a brown plastic tomato, mustard in a condiment set with malt vinegar, white pepper and sticky salt. Then there was High Tea: packet tomato soup heavily slurped, grey gravy with little white lumps and some meat fibres in it accompanied by dead cabbage and runny boiled potatoes. Sweet was a scoop of vanilla ice-cream, a peach slice and a wafer. Bel smiled and gulped like the red-nosed tourists with the squawking children and the teenagers in ear-muff stereos. I'd always hated Aunty Esme's. To see Bel not only take it in her stride, but to seem to be actually enjoying the chaos, the dumped plates, the chocolate-coloured tea in see-through cups and the James Last muzak was unbelievable.

'You're enjoying this!' I accused her.

'Why not? It's a holiday. It's free. It's a laugh!' she shrugged. 'Hey, listen . . . why don't we cheat? Let's stay here for a week, then go back and tell Terry we made it to Scotland. It needn't cost us much and . . .'

'You're joking!' I exploded.

'Er . . . 'course I am!' she stammered.

But I had my doubts. After tea, Bel dressed in yet another set of plumage: coral jacket, turquoise pedal-pushers and a pair of particularly violent red-and-white high heels with cut-outs and bows. I put on my black T-shirt with jeans and black sandals to go out on the town. I walked by Bel's side as she sashayed down the Golden Mile, boogying to the blast of pop music surging from souvenir and rock shops, amusement arcades and T-shirt stalls, begging chips from tattooed grinning thugs who smirked and winked and followed us until it became obvious that we weren't going to share their cans of lager with them.

'Isn't it great here, Meg?' she kept saying. 'Just smell the sea air and the vinegar and the onions. It's fantastic. I love it.'

'So what're you trying to say?' I asked warily, in the end.

'Oh . . . nothing. Shame we can't splash out and spend the whole of our fivers, here and now. I could buy one of those rock dummies for our Winston, you could get off with one of these passing fellas, and I could sneak off to phone Terry when you weren't looking . . . Joke. Joke, Meg. Don't be a pain. Live a little. Here . . .' she grinned, marching up to a little kid with a polystyrene tray swimming in ketchup and vinegar. 'Give us a chip, tight-arse! Ta!'

She grabbed two, and pushed one into my mouth. It was limp, greasy and raw in the middle. Cuisine Blackpool. Good plain English food, Aunty Esme calls it. Then Bel linked my arm and led me off towards the Pleasure Beach.

'Live a little!' she laughed, again. 'We're free!'

Free. To the right the sea lay, slate-grey and lace under a mackerel sky. Lights twinkled in strung ribbons above our heads. Flowers, in bright patterns, glowed down the wide promenades. There were horse-drawn carriages, kids screaming, laughter, music, ice-creams, candy-floss like pink fog, and there was me, resisting it all, too busy thinking just to be. My steps fell in with Bel's, my hips rocked to the rhythm. It felt good. Fried onions, limp chips, spitting doughnuts smelt good. Big dippers did the bump and the grind, waltzers danced, guns fired. It brought back memories of when I was a little kid, and all this was wonderland. Bel was right. It was a laugh.

She nudged me, and pointed to two hulking youths in low-slung jeans and close-fitting T-shirts.

'Listen in!' Bel whispered, pulling me along to follow them through the crowds.

'What?'

'Listen to these two. Just listen. It might come in handy,' she hissed.

'Jesus H.,' one of the fat guys complained, staring up at the upside-down and inside-out mass of steel girders that constituted the 'Ride of Death'. 'Jesus H., is that all the machine can do? It's for bairns. It's no' for grown men. It's no' worth a pound of good money, Derek.'

'Huh?' I asked Bel.

'They're from Scotland, aren't they? Just listen!' she said.

'Don't look now, Kevin, but there's two lassies behind us . . .' Derek whispered.

I kicked Bel gently in the shins as the two turned round slowly. Bel grinned, stupidly.

'Excuse me for asking,' she murmured. 'But my friend and I were thinking of going to Scotland in the next few days, like, and I heard you talking and . . . well, could you describe Scotland to us?'

'Scotland?' Derek asked, scratching his sandy crew-cut.

'Scotland?' Kevin asked, screwing up his tight eyes even more tightly. 'Well, we wouldn't really know. There's a lot of houses there, so I've heard.'

'And hills. There's hills, Kevin,' Derek told him.

'Oh, aye. I remember a wee hill or two. But we're from Birmingham. I only went to Scotland the once, for a Cup match.'

'I went when I was a bairn, once, as well, Kevin,' Derek said, searching his memory.

'Well, thanks anyway!' Bel said, stifling her giggles, and dragged me away from the two, into the crowd, leaving them scratching their heads still and shrugging with disbelief.

'What was all that about?' I panted through the laughter.

'Oh, just an idea I had. Nothing really . . .' Bel murmured, sobering up. 'Don't think about it, right. Just don't think about it . . .'

'It's what you said earlier, isn't it? It's that idea you had about staying here and pretending we'd been to Scotland? You thought if you could make Terry think we'd been to Scotland and met some Scottish lads, and came home talking about heather and haggis and wee hills . . .! Honest, Bel!'

'OK, OK, but Terry says . . .'

Her voice faltered.

'Terry said?' I prompted.

'Oh, nothing . . .'

She shrugged me off and marched from the Pleasure Beach, across the road, through the honking traffic, to the quiet side of the street, the promenade and the darkening distant sea. She flung herself on the nearest bench, and I sat down next to her.

'Fairs make me sick,' she snapped.

'What's up? What's wrong?' I asked.

'Terry's up,' she said, quietly. 'I shouldn't've thought of him. It's a problem.'

'What is?'

'Fancying him. Someone like him. Like he eats me alive, Meg. I think about him all the time, even when I'm pretending not to. I think of Terry, and it's like belonging to someone, like as if you're their bike, or their favourite LP or their best jeans. You're not you. You're just a thing that belongs. It's no good. But it is. What I'm trying to say is that I miss him already. We're every night in that bloody cellar, and he's moaning about the hole in his kecks, or his last fifty pence, and I'm bored, but I can't leave because I love him, and now I can't love this because I keep making plans for cheating him and getting back to him and being bored mindless again. Now does that make sense?'

'No,' I admitted, grinning.

'It doesn't, does it?' she grinned back. 'I'm scared of getting too far away from him. I thought we could go back the day after tomorrow and say we saw Scotland, give us a day out in Southport. But that's not what this is all about, is it?'

'No.'

'Remember, Meg? Remember that first night? You said, "Let's try down there. It might be better than sitting at home revising 'Dallas'." So we went down, and there was Terry, sitting in the corner with Benno and Yob, and he yelled over. At you, eh? He shouted something, at you, something dead sarky, but you know what? When I looked at him I knew, straight off, I knew he was the one for me. He had that stupid Rasta hat on, didn't he? Made him look like he'd walked into a Neapolitan ice-cream.

But . . . that's how it is. I fancy Neapolitan ice-creams. I wish you could understand, Meg.'

'And why shouldn't I?' I muttered, crossly. 'Think I've never been in love? What about this ex of mine we're supposed to be staying with tomorrow? Why d'you think I've been a bit off today? I've been wondering how it's going to be, what I'm going to say to him, how he'll look, now.'

Couples walked past us in a moonglow under the starry lights, coiled together like pipecleaners. If Bel could make a big issue out of her romance, I wasn't going to sit back and think of myself as some poor unloved creature. It was time to lay it on with a trowel.

'So,' Bel grinned, her head on one side. 'We've got to the bottom of today's big mystery, have we? Go on, then. Tell me about him. What's he like?'

'The usual. Tall and dark and incredibly handsome,' I lied.

I tried to recall the face on the sticky photograph. It was, as far as I could remember, a quite unremarkable face. It had two insignificant grey eyes and a gummy smile, salty hair blown into awkward spikes, and the occasional spot. And Peter himself had been pigeontoed, a little bandy, slightly smaller than I was. Perhaps in the intervening year or so he'd grown into something I could pass off as an attractive ex-boyfriend. I just hoped he'd grown.

'He's very mature, not like Terry,' I invented. 'He's considerate, intellectual, really –' I prayed he'd grown out of the *Beano* jokes '– but not the sort of boy you'd be attracted to immediately, if you know what I mean. Not sort of obviously and superficially hunky-looking. Unusual.'

'Mmm,' Bel smiled. 'I'm looking forward to meeting him.'

My shoulders sagged. I kicked the paving stones with the toe of my sandal and hoped that I'd covered myself for the disappointment of seeing Pete again.

'It's going to be OK,' Bel smiled, almost to herself.

'What is?'

'This is. This. It's going to be an adventure. It's something smart-arse Terry wouldn't dare to do, isn't it? I'm sorry for being scared and pathetic. I'm not going to think about Terry again, promise. I'll just phone him when we get back, and you can phone your whatshisname to let him know we're arriving on his doorstep tomorrow. Your Aunty Esme'll let us use her phone, won't she?'

'Yeah,' I agreed dubiously. Something still nagged inside. I hoped it wasn't jealousy. 'So we're on, are we? Uncle Wilf says he'll give us a lift at six if we really want to go to Haverigg. Are we going?'

'Are we going? Are we going! 'Course we're going! I wouldn't miss seeing the love of your life, now would I? So what the hell're we doing, sitting here like a couple of dead whelks. Let's go! Let's do it.' Her voice thickened into a mock American accent and rose into a singing falsetto. 'Places to go, people to meet,' she sang, springing from the bench, pulling me up after her. 'You do the backing track!'

'Ba-ba-ba-loo-ba,' I sang, obediently clicking back through the staggering crowds. Men with hats and sticks, and women with neat grey curls, turned to watch us. We smiled back at them, dancing to the music we were slaughtering all the way back to Aunty Esme's.

I stayed outside the lounge, in the hallway, examining the faded red carpet and the vouchers for fifty pence off Tower Ballroom admission, while Bel croaked lovingly into the phone to Terry. I tried not to hear. I tried to hear myself talking in the same husky, desiring tones to little Pete, but it didn't seem appropriate somehow.

'Finished,' Bel shouted, finally. 'Come on down! It's your turn for Sexy Secrets.'

'Sshh! Esme might hear you,' I whispered.

Shakily, I dialled Pete's number, wondering what on earth I was going to say. Bel stood wriggling in her rainbow colours, all excitement and encouragement.

'It's ringing,' I managed to say.

It rang. And rang. And rang.

After five minutes, I replaced the receiver, slowly. Bel and I stared at each other in the quiet while bells rang, still, inside my head.

'So . . .?' she murmured.

'They're probably out for the evening,' I suggested dully.

'Probably. Probably.'

'So?'

'Wagons roll! Let's just turn up on the doorstep with the milk. You can throw stones up at his bedroom window and do a Romeo and Juliet scene. Very romantic!'

'We take a chance?' I asked.

'Terry reckons Blackpool's as far as we'll get. Sod him. We take a chance,' Bel spat, angrily. 'Thinks he knows it all. We'll show him.'

Chapter Four

Uncle Wilf banged on our bedroom door at five o'clock. His excuse for the ungodly hour was that he wanted to drive us to the Lake District and get back in time to help Aunty Esme with the seven o'clock breakfasts, but that schedule went right out of the window. Bel took some persuading that five o'clock was daytime on some body clocks. Then we had the argument about whether or not she'd be able to carry her house-sized suitcase on the trek up to Scotland. Eventually she compromised a little by borrowing Uncle Wilf's old Army kitbag, a huge tattered sausage of a bag with a thousand and one zipped compartments, filling that with as many clothes as she could cram into it in an hour, and finally tottering downstairs with it clattering alongside her. As a final act of defiance she wore her stupid red-and-white stilt-heeled shoes, and a sulk. The rest of her clothes were left at Aunty Esme's for picking up on the way back.

Uncle Wilf sulked, too, lighting up his pipe as soon as we'd been pushed into the car at half-past six, and muttering under his breath about women and traffic. Smoke and a brooding silence filled the car. The brooding was all mine. I was busy rehearsing my reunion with the love of my life, a boy I couldn't quite remember. I blinked back sleep and smarting eyes, trying to take some comfort from the brilliant gold and greens of the countryside, and the humped hills leaning down river estuaries and into the sea.

Uncle Wilf had got it into his mind that we were going to Ulverston. Three wrong turnings and my preoccupied and startled last-minute changes of instruction as to direction did little to improve his mood. Haverigg eventually appeared on signposts. I perfected a 'Hello, Pete. Guess who?' routine as we swerved round hairpin bends. Bel groaned, coughed impressively, and wound down both the back windows.

'This what you want?' Uncle Wilf asked, finally, pulling up by a stream tangled with willowherb which opened out into a wide boulder-strewn bay and some pale sun-washed houses.

'Thanks,' I smiled, nervously. 'It'll do.'

He looked at his watch, ostentatiously, while we struggled out. Or at least, I struggled out, sensing an explosion from the driver's seat at any moment, and pulled at my haversack, then at the sausage bag that was occupying most of the room in the back seat. Just as the car was pulling away, Bel opened the nearside door and fell straight into a passing hiker. He crumpled. Bel's heel became lodged in a grating and she crumpled, too. The car sped away, leaving the two bodies spluttering on the verge.

'Why don't you look where you're going?' Bel screamed at the hiker, venting all her pent-up fury on him, while he tried to help her to her feet. 'Look at my knee! There's nearly blood on it!'

He seemed confused by her onslaught, smiled awkwardly, and tried to retrieve his own rucksack from the ditch.

'Sorry!' he muttered.

'It wasn't your fault. Don't apologize to her. She's

in a foul mood. That's why she's wearing those ridiculous shoes . . .' I started to explain before I realized that, to a stranger, the explanation would probably be more of a tangle than the original incident.

'They're not ridiculous. They cost twenty-nine ninety-nine, Megan Griffiths, and now I've scuffed the heel, and I don't know how I'm going to pretend I did all that damage in Blackpool!' Bel shot back at me.

I blinked. The sun threw haloes round the hiker's head. He was silhouetted against it, a tall blond boy in jeans and a T-shirt, impossibly tanned, smiling a very white smile, dimple in his chin, bedroll and rucksack now firmly on his back.

'I'm . . .' he started to say, hand outstretched.

'Omigod, you're American!' Bel shuddered. 'Might've known. You're a serviceman, right? And when you're not hiking round the country, you drive nuclear missiles. Your hobbies are chewing gum, and pushing girls over, swimming in your daddy's oil-well and having your teeth straightened. I know your type!'

'Take no notice of her . . .' I stammered, embarrassed. 'She watches too much television. Really she thinks you're a film producer, and she's auditioning for a part in a video nasty, aren't you, Bel?' Out of the corner of my mouth I whispered, 'What's got into you? Behave!'

'I'm Michael O'Connor, from Washington. Student. I'm hitching round the UK,' he smiled at me, obviously amused by the flak that was passing between me and Bel.

'Megan Griffiths, from Liverpool. And this used to be my best friend. Her name's Annabel. She's OK when you get to know her. After ten o'clock in the morning she turns into a person,' I smiled back.

He was OK, in a conventional sort of way – clean-cut, stereotyped, muscular and bright-eyed. But there was a wicked twinkle in his grey-blue eyes that I quite liked. If he'd been five feet smaller and two feet wider, he'd've made quite a passable leprechaun.

'I hate to interrupt you two when you're obviously having such an enthralling time, but we really must go. Remember, Meg?' Bel smiled, in a sick sugary way. 'You're on your way to see your boyfriend, aren't you?'

I glared at her but she just smiled more widely.

'Maybe I'll see you around,' Michael O'Connor said, shaking my hand, and offering his hand to Bel who ignored it and stooped to pick up her kitbag instead.

'Have a nice day!' she called after him in a mock American accent.

I watched him go, and shook my head at Bel.

'So what was that all about?' I asked.

'I'm hungry. I eat people when I'm hungry. Especially Americans. Terry can't stand them, but I think they're quite sweet – sweet enough to give you tooth decay, at any rate. So, I want my breakfast. I want double bacon, three eggs, potato cakes and black pudding. D'you think this Pete guy loves you enough to feed your friend?' she asked, plaintively, tottering along at my side.

'He wasn't bad,' I muttered.

'Pete?'

'No. That American.'

'Come off it, Meg! They're all big-headed and loud-mouthed. That one was just conning us into believing he was different. And shouldn't your mind be on Pete? The Big Romance that was supposed to be. Or were you just having me on when you were going on about him last night?'

'No!' I protested, too quickly.

I led the way along the main street of dull cottages. The sun had the bitter-lemon tang of summer early mornings, and gulls swooped and called over our heads. My legs felt heavy and watery. I knew that this was something they didn't want to do. Pete? I couldn't even remember the colour of his hair.

I trembled to a halt outside number forty-three, an anonymous silent house like the others in the street. I tried to imagine those two or three silly letters I'd written dropping through the narrow mailbox in that blue front door. It was a good solid front door, standing squarely between four empty windows like dead eyes.

'This it?' Bel panted, negotiating the cobblestones behind me.

'This *was* it,' I told her, pointing.

In the tiny front garden, stuck into the lavender and sea-pinks of the rockery, was a leaning sign. 'For sale' it read. Plastered across it was a sticker, 'Sold'. Bel didn't follow the arc of my finger. Blindly she stumbled to the door, banged on the doorknocker and rang the bell, repeatedly. The sound echoed hollowly.

A woman with hairgrips in her fringe poked her head from behind the nets in an upstairs window next door.

'Did you want something?' she asked, petulantly.

'Not something. Someone. My friend, here, she's looking for her fiancé,' Bel shouted back.

'Fiancé?' the woman queried.

'Pete. His name's Pete Hanson,' Bel explained. I buried my face in my rucksack and didn't know whether to laugh or cry.

'The Hansons've flitted. Two weeks ago. Gone to Bromley . . . I think that's down south. But he never had no fiancé, not as far as I knew, and me and Elsie Hanson were like that.' She crossed her fingers to show the degree of intimacy. 'How could he have a fiancé, and him only sixteen last April? Not out of school yet,' the woman shouted, mystified.

'Sixteen?' I exploded. 'He said he was sixteen that summer! He looked sixteen, Bel. Honest!'

'Baby-snatcher!' she giggled quietly at me. 'Thanks, anyway, missus. You've been very helpful.'

She could hardly pick up her kitbag for laughing.

'Mature, she says,' she chuckled, leading the way back down the road. 'The Real Thing, she says. And him only just out of nappies! Sorry, Meg, honest, I didn't mean to show you up, and I'm sorry I'm laughing, but you have to admit it's a bit funny. How did it feel, going out with a boy who's a couple of months younger than you? You know, the last time I went out with a boy my own age, I was seven. Aw, come 'e'd, Meg. Come on. Come on,' she laughed, slinging her arm round my shoulders, trying to make me feel better about it. I slid from under her arm and walked behind her.

I couldn't bear it. The shame and embarrassment of having embroidered that pathetic holiday romance to try to impress Bel had devastated me. I couldn't understand what was wrong with me. Was I so desperate that I'd tried to make Bel believe that he was attractive, old, wise, instead of a stupid kid? Was I totally pathetic? I felt foolish, gawky beside the worldly Bel, like a child myself, too young for a real boy like Terry. Far too naive. And what if Pete Hanson *had* been at home? What if he *had* answered the door? Would that have been better or worse? I couldn't decide. I'd made him sound so important. He was just a faded memory.

My eyes stung.

'Sand in my eyes,' I explained to Bel when she glanced back and saw me rubbing at them.

'Just one little problem here, Meg,' Bel called over her shoulder. 'Now we've lost your toy-boy, we're a bit short on breakfast and somewhere to sleep tonight. Did that thought enter your head?'

'Mmm,' I nodded. That thought was trying to enter. Other things were holding it back.

'So? Any ideas?' she asked.

'Bacon sarnies, on the beach? I could make a fire. We'll buy a loaf, and I've got some pre-packed bacon in here. There's a water-tap down there, next to the paddling pool, so we can have some instant hot chocolate, too. Is that OK?' I mumbled. I felt tired now, and very hungry. I always get hungry when I'm really upset about something.

Bel suggested that she bought the bread, while I collected wood and started the fire. We stood on the concrete walkway in front of the tarry beach, selecting a sheltered spot by the dunes, and Bel handed over her kitbag to me while she raced off to find a shop.

Solitude gave me the opportunity to cry. There was no one on the empty shore, except a dog foraging on the edges of the estuary. I stumbled along with the bags, sobbing noisily to myself, dumped them in the agreed spot, and kicked stones as I collected drift-wood. It didn't help. Bel, I knew, would take the opportunity to sneer about Pete Hanson at every low point. The indignity of my position had already put a spring into her wobbly step and a giggle into her blue mood. Perhaps some day we could both laugh at the memory. Meanwhile, I let the tears out.

Chapter Five

Bel didn't mention Pete again, not that day. She returned from the shops like the old Bel, determined to restore my shattered morale. I was hunched over a meagre attempt at a fire, but together we collected more wood, built a windbreak with stones, and soon had quite a professional camp-fire glowing. We toasted the bacon by hanging it in front of the heat on forks. The fat sizzled and spat into the flames under the billy-can. Apart from the problem with sand on the bread, the sandwiches were crunchily fantastic. It was almost midday when we'd finished coaxing the fire, eating and drinking. The sun blazed from a cornflower sky, the beach had sprouted deckchairs and canvas windbreaks, men in rolled-up trousers, women in one-piece bathing suits, cricket and soccer tournaments, sandcastles, Grand Canals, kite-flying and horse-riding. Bel and I, a distance away from the main action, changed into bikinis under the cover of towels and fell asleep in the sun, prodded awake occasionally by buzzing flies, screeching gulls, showers of sand from the kids sliding down the dunes, and passing ghetto-blasters.

By four o'clock, awake and munching on the mint-cake my mum had packed into the haversack, we discussed the next move. We pored over the map, discussing our route.

'We could head up this coast,' I suggested.

'Up here?' Bel shuddered, pointing at the power-station on the coast to the north. 'Isn't that the place where the fish tick? That's a nuclear fallout zone, Meg. I'm not even sure whether I'm safe here. I didn't realize we were so close to You-know-where. Listen, if I start to glow, you're my best mate, you'll be the first to tell me, won't you? Don't let me hear it from someone else. I'd hate to get back home and find myself going transparent in the disco.'

'You and five hundred others,' I told her, gesturing towards the crowded part of the beach.

'OK, OK, let's say we're safeish here. Safe enough to stay the night. We could sleep in the dunes. We'd've stayed here anyway if things had turned out different, so let's just waste the rest of the day and make out like it's a holiday. Right?'

'Right,' I agreed. 'And tomorrow morning?'

'We could go back across our tracks, as far as Broughton, then Ambleside and Kendal, or up there, Grasmere way. We get back on the motorway and head for Scotland,' she decided.

Bel was always impressive when she was in one of these instant-reaction moods. Sometimes she seemed lazy, too eager to find an excuse to quote Terry, or lean on him. But I think she knew that. I think that's what she'd been complaining about the previous night.

'Sure you want to go to Scotland?' I asked her.

'Isn't that what this Girl-Guide stunt's all about?' she grinned.

At six, we ran briefly into the sea to wash some of the sand off. The tide was out, the sand soggy, cold, mined with holes that someone's dog had made, and bright with razor shells and cockle shells. We ran miles, it seemed, through the cooling evening breeze, to a grey sea that took our breath away. We splashed and played kids' games, giggling stupidly, goose-bumped and terrified by floating jellyfish. The run back to the dunes seemed to take even longer. The sun had lost most of its heat by the time we returned to our bags and impromptu camp. Dried and sticky in sweaters, we dug a hole in a nearby dune, wrapped our bags in polythene sheeting and buried them, so that we could spend the night on the town.

There wasn't much town to spend much of a night on. We'd already decided to splash out on chips for the evening meal with a tin of sardines that I'd put in my jeans' pocket. It was as well we hadn't decided on anything more ambitious. There wasn't anything more ambitious to do.

There was a children's playground, though, on the edge of the sand, next to the slimy paddling pool. We whooped it up on the swings, hung upside-down on the climbing frame, see-sawed until babies complained to their mothers about us, and tried to slide down the tacky slide. The children's playground was the high spot of the evening. From the highest arc of the swing, the cliffs beyond seemed to be pitted with derelict mine buildings. The bright houses along the estuary looked dull and flaking in the evening light, their stucco crumbling, balconies leaning. As night drew in, the neglect looked almost threatening, more threatening in its open windy spaces than the dark alleys of Toxteth.

But perhaps I was programmed to see desolation in the town. Perhaps the desolation wasn't around me but inside, in the place where my pride had been pummelled earlier in the day. I felt alone, despite Bel's singing on the swing next to me, despite her giggling good humour and careful avoidance of references to Pete Hanson. Or Terry.

I was grateful for her company, and her concern, thankful when finally she launched herself from the swing in mid-flight and beckoned me to do the same.

'Time to eat. Playtime over, kids,' she shouted at me through the darkness. Arm in arm we clattered down the cobbled street to the chip shop. Two or three Cumbrian hard cases posed outside in studded bomber jackets, next to one motorbike. A couple of girls, trying to look equally hard, shared a can of Coke and snarled at us when we pushed by into the vinegary warmth.

The chips, though, were mountainous, hot and crisp, fried in lard and wrapped in wads of newspaper. Bel showered them with vinegar and salt, and we sat outside, on a bench, sharing them and foraging inside the half-opened sardine can which, as usual, wouldn't yield any further no matter how hard I turned the key. We had to bang the can to release the sardines on to our pile of chips. The bike boys sneered. Their girls muttered.

'Shouldn't be allowed in.'

'Send 'em back to the jungle.'

'And fancy them coming here – on holiday!'

Bel sucked hard on a chip and stared out the girl in the pink short skirt and denim jacket who was doing most of the muttering.

'Are you talking about us?' she asked quietly.

I liked the fact that she said 'us'.

'Because, if you are, we're not on holiday. We've just moved in,' she continued, just as quietly.

The boy on the bike stopped revving the tiny engine. The girl's jaw dropped.

'We moved in down East Street today. You'll be seeing a lot more of us in the future, because . . . well, there're a lot more of us. There's my mum and dad,' Bel counted, her mouth full of chips, 'then there's our Delroy who's six foot seven and twenty stone. He's in the scrap-metal business, know what I mean? He collects iron bars and turns any motorbikes he sees into scrap metal. Then there's Maurice and Lucas and Ellis – they're practising to be urban terrorists, not that they've got much to practise on here, but they'll have a good try. Winston's the north-west heavyweight tag-wrestling champion. And Denny . . .' she took another chip and waggled it around to cool it while her audience stared, dumbstruck, ' . . . he's just been released but he'll be back inside, we reckon, within a week or so. He just can't help mugging bikers. Our Richie's going the same way, too. Me and our Ruthie haven't been in much trouble, recently, but Delroy's fiancée here,' she nodded at me, 'says she'll teach us the ropes. Of course Kevin, Darren, Dean and Wayne are still at school, sometimes, so they've still got some living to do. We'll try not to make life difficult for you lot, as long as you don't make life difficult for us – is it a deal?'

By this time I was choking on the last chip, struggling to keep my face straight. The hard mob was gawping. Bel scrunched the newspaper up in one hand, and threw it expertly into the litter bin. Five pairs of eyes goggled.

'I said, is it a deal?' Bel repeated, standing, smoothing down her canary trousers and hotching her shoulders inside the red check jacket.

'Er . . . yeah . . . suppose,' one of the bikers muttered, in confusion.

'Keep out of our space, right?' she insisted, walking straight at them. I followed. The boys jumped in the gutter to let us pass. I don't think they'd quite worked Bel or her crazy story out, and were hedging their bets.

We walked tall and rigid, listening hard to their frantic whispering and nervous chuntering, until we'd rounded the corner on to the beach path. Then we both exploded into hysterics. I thought I was going to be sick with laughter. Chips and sardines churned in my stomach.

'Did you see the one with "kill" tattooed on his fingers?' Bel screeched. 'He was thinking so hard, he was crunching his Coke can!'

'And the girl with the Monsters of Rock badge was nearly wetting herself,' I added. 'God, you were brilliant, Bel! Where did you learn to do that?'

Her laughter died suddenly.

'Where d'you think? How often d'you think I've had to put up with that kind of hassle, eh? You just give them what they want and watch them turn whiter than white. It's a pity I can't do the same, sometimes.'

'Sorry, Bel,' I murmured.

'What for? We're mates, aren't we?' she laughed, digging me in the ribs and grinning. 'You're all right, kiddo. It's some of them other buggers. Now, how're we going to find our bags? Just look at the darkness out there!'

We'd arrived at the edge of the beach. Distantly, the sea shrugged on to the black shore. Dunes humped like spoil-heaps. Small dark shapes swooped from the night sky.

'Should've brought a torch,' I stammered.

'No use thinking of that now, is there? Come on. Let's use our jungle cunning,' Bel giggled, grabbing my hand, leading me along the beach towards the dunes. 'I remember it was by the seventh breakwater. And there was a sewage outlet just before the gap in the dunes – here, smell it. We're on the right track, Sherlock!'

'Six . . . seven . . .' I murmured, counting the shadowed breakwaters as we passed. 'So – up here?'

'Looks about right. Now look for the stick we planted over the hole.'

It took us half an hour digging, searching on our hands and knees, cutting arms, hands and faces on marram grass before finally locating the bags. We could just about make out the shape of things, but, as we tugged to find towels, polythene sheeting and my blanket, sand slid in everywhere. Bel made a hollow in the sand, used her sausage bag as a pillow, and covered herself in towels. I wrapped myself in my blanket and polythene sheeting like a cocoon, put my haversack under my head, and closed my eyes.

But it was cold. The night was full of strange sounds. Creatures padded or slinked or rustled past us. The moon threw ghostly shadows. I heaved my rucksack and cocoon closer to Bel's hollow.

'Can't sleep,' she whispered.

'Me neither,' I admitted. 'And I've just thought of something . . . What did you do with the change from that fiver I gave you to buy bread with?'

'I bought the chips, didn't I?'

'Yeah, but that was only fifty pence.'

'I've got the other two pounds something in my pocket,' Bel muttered, sleepily.

'Two pounds something! There should be more than that!' I breathed.

'Well, I had to buy rock for our Winston, and something for my mum and dad. I bought them a toffee kipper.'

'Bel!'

'Look, *I'm* supposed to be on holiday in Blackpool, not shivering on this beach in Ku Klux Klan country. Right? They'll expect prezzies, so I've got to take prezzies home. Why don't you stop worrying and go to sleep?'

'But we've only got . . .'

'We've got enough left. We'll manage. We've managed so far, haven't we? Pretty well, I reckon. I think I'm starting to enjoy this,' she yawned.

'Are you?' I smiled to myself.

'Not half as much as the furry thing that's just crawled under these towels with me – OK, don't panic, it's just crawled out again. It's coming over to you, I reckon. Sleep well.'

'Thanks,' I said, closing my eyes, imagining furry things with Terry's gap-toothed smile, gnawing at me.

Chapter Six

We cooked bacon sandwiches again for breakfast before shaking sand from everything, packing and striking camp next morning. Most of the morning had gone before we set out on the road to Broughton. I was worried about the money Bel had frittered away, but too sleepy to argue over it. Whirling swifts and gulls had woken us from only four or five hours' fitful sleep and my eyes felt gritty. My freckles were burning, too, after the previous day's sunbathing. I knew I was niggly.

'Let's walk down this road until we get a lift to Ambleside,' I yawned.

'No way. We're going to sit on the pavement, right here, while we hitch,' Bel insisted. 'You don't think I'm going to walk anywhere in these shoes, do you?'

Her feet were still crammed into the red-and-white stilts.

'Haven't you brought any other shoes?' I wailed.

'Yeah, three pairs. But they're not as comfy as these. I've got my plimmies for emergencies, but you can't hitch in plimmies, can you? No one'll give a lift to a girl in plimmies.'

So we sat on the hot pavement, and waited. The sun was too high and sticky. Flies hummed in some willowherb that hung in sickly pink plumes over the cracked mudbank of the estuary. There was a terrifying stillness. A bus trundled past.

'I dream about this sort of thing sometimes,' I murmured, leaning back on my haversack. 'I dream it's the end of the world, but I didn't hear the warning, and I'm miles away from home. Everyone's dead but me, but I don't know that, and I don't know why I'm not dead.'

'Perhaps you are,' Bel rambled, 'only you don't know. Perhaps you're a ghost. But only in your dream, not in real life. You'd have to *be* something, or the dream wouldn't happen, would it? So, you think you're alive because you're writing the dream. Terry explained all that to me, once. He's got these theories, really complicated ones. He says . . . Hey, I forgot to phone him!'

'Later,' I sighed. 'Phone him later. If I ever wake up out of this dream I don't want you to be in a phone box. And there's a car coming.'

It wasn't a car. It was a rickety bread van, hurtling round the corner. Bel and I jumped to our feet and flagged it down, desperately.

'Ambleside?' I asked the grey-haired driver.

'Only as far as the crossroads beyond Broughton, but you're welcome. Back's full of trays, so watch yourselves. Climb in, if you can,' he smiled.

Climbing in was straightforward for me. It was more painful for Bel in her tight black-and-white spotted skirt. Finally, I dragged her in, so that she was lying face down, nose in a tray of sliced bread, as the van pulled away.

The journey was horrific. The van keeled round bends, bread rolls bounced, loaves slid and skated. Bel and I hung on to the racking, and to our bags, and watched the scenery – walls, trees, streams, bridges and hills – blur into a kind of grey pea soup.

'This man's a maniac!' Bel gulped, trying to slide away from a tray of French sticks that were attacking her.

'Delivering bread's probably just a hobby for him. He probably drives stock-cars for a living,' I grinned, holding tight.

'After dark, he probably transforms into an ultrasonic vampire,' Bel panted.

'Maybe he sliced all this bread with his own teeth,' I suggested.

'Maybe we'll never reach Broughton . . .'

'Maybe we'll reach it, but we'll be sliced, too, by the time we get there.'

'Should we leap out the next time he slows down?' Bel asked.

'You first,' I said.

When the brakes were finally slammed on, both of us catapulted out of the back. Bel landed on her sausage bag. The seams, already weak, gave way, and jackets and trousers spilled out into the road.

'Broughton crossroads,' the driver said, proudly. 'That's the road you want for Ambleside.'

'I'm choosing the next lift,' Bel moaned, trying to cram her belongings back into the yawning bag.

We sat on the grass verge, trying to hold the bag together. Sheep chomped in the field behind us. As far as the eye could see there were only dry stone walls, sheep, tangled wire, trees, hills and cow-parsley.

And a brilliant red Jaguar XJ6.

I saw it first, when it was a speck on the horizon.

'I choose this one!' Bel squealed, leaping up to follow its progress. 'It's coming this way. It's getting closer . . . It's . . . Never!'

'What?' I demanded. 'What?'

I stood up, too, leaving the bag to empty its contents once more, on the verge.

'Just look at that. It's stopped. Some nerd with an orange rucksack just stopped it and got in. Someone just nicked my lift!'

She was beside herself with anger, leaping around maniacally as the car sped past us, stamping her stilts in fury. Then she froze, and stared. I froze, too. The nerd in the back seat waved at us and smiled a perfect blond smile.

'You saw who that was?' Bel breathed.

'Him. The American.'

'Right. Right, that does it! I was prepared to put my prejudices aside, but that does it! That's typical, that is. They come here and they nick things that belong to us!' she raved, sounding suspiciously like the bikers in Haverigg. 'And then they smile.'

'He's got a nice smile,' I said, almost to myself.

'Nice smile! Nice smile! I'd have a nice smile if I was riding along in a Jag!' Bel raved, inconsolable. 'Right, Meg! Here's another car. I'll sort this one out.'

She raced out into the middle of the road, waving madly. The car screeched to a halt.

'. . . See, we've got to get to Carlisle quickly, because her mum's on the danger list . . .' I could hear her wheedling as I staggered up, hugging the sausage bag to me like a dancing partner.

'Get in,' she hissed. 'And look tragic. Your mum's on the blink in Carlisle hospital!'

'We're only going as far as Ambleside,' the driver stammered, looking towards his wife for confirmation.

'Well . . .' Bel sighed, almost irritably. 'I suppose that'll just have to do. Let's hope the life-support system can keep her going until we get another lift from Ambleside.'

She pushed me and the bags into the back seat and crawled in afterwards, pausing only to pick up a fuchsia T-shirt that was hanging half in and half out of the bag.

The driver and his wife communicated only in smiles, nods, movements of the eyebrows, occasional hand signals. The car was smooth and comfortable, piano music oozed from the stereo, but I felt awkward, compromised by Bel's lies, and stared out of the window, disowning her. Hills became steeper, green turned to grey-blue as we rose into fell-land and tumbled into tangles of leaves when we rolled into river valleys. There were glints of blue water through traceries of branches, and houses, built of the same dark stone as the mean seaside houses we were escaping from, looked portly and substantial, with rolling lawns and twinkling windows. Hikers stretched in lines down the busier roads, most dressed like German goat girls in shorts, knee-length socks and heavy walking-boots. Bel shuddered each time we passed another beaming crocodile. It wasn't her idea of fun.

At Windermere, the car slowed. Traffic trundled bumper to bumper through the grey crowded streets.

'This'll do!' Bel shrieked suddenly. 'You can drop us off here. Thanks very much.'

'But I thought . . .' the woman frowned, craning her neck back to stare at us.

'My mistake. I just remembered. It's Windermere hospital, not Carlisle hospital. Come on, Meg. Let's hope you can pull her out of the coma, again!'

She tugged at me until I almost fell out of the car. I couldn't understand this latest impulse, but muttered my own thanks, and cringed with embarrassment when I saw the bewilderment in the couple's eyes.

'She's not very well, my friend,' I whispered to them by way of weak explanation.

Bel tugged at me again until I was free of the car, then slammed the door and waved to the couple. The fuchsia T-shirt, trapped for ever in the car door, waved back.

'What was *that* all about?' Bel demanded loudly as soon as she'd pulled me on to the pavement.

'I was just about to ask you the same question! Why the sudden change of mind? Why have we got out here, in this tourist hell-hole? What're we doing, Bel?'

'I saw a chip shop with a phone box outside, and it gave me an idea, that's all,' she said. 'You get the chips. I'll phone Terry. Give us fifty pence.'

'No,' I said angrily.

'Aw, go on. I've got to tell him we're halfway to Scotland, haven't I? Rub it in a bit, eh? And I'll get him to go round our house and let my mum know I'm still having a wonderful time in Blackpool. Go on, Meg. You know what my dad's like. Best set his mind at rest. And, tell you what, since you're doing me a favour, I'll do you one as well. I'll phone Terry *and* get the chips. You sit on that bench and take the weight off your fat legs for a few minutes. And hold my bag tight. Gottit?'

She looked so helpless, I had to give in. I sat, obediently, on the bench, surrounded by our possessions. In the distance crowds queued to cross the blue mirror of water, half-hidden by trees. I liked the look of that water: still, hidden depths, obscured by hanging leaves. I wanted to buy a postcard view of it, one of those displayed on the shop stand just an arm's reach from the bench, and send it, with love, to someone. Anyone.

I swallowed hard. Tiredness brings miseries to

the surface. It stirs up emotions that are best left still, hidden, and obscured by snide jokes.

Bel came out of the chip shop, cradling a bag of chips, her mouth full.

'These cost forty, so I only had ten-pence worth with Terry, but it was worth it! He sounded that put out! I reckon he thought we'd've only got as far as Birkenhead by now and be on our way back.'

I tried to grab some chips before she ate them all. Each time I reached, she moved the bag closer to her. We fought over the crispy bits in the bottom. Bel won. Didn't she always?

'It's nice here,' Bel sighed.

'Except for up there.' I pointed towards the sky. Scudding white clouds banked across the blue, approaching the sun. A chill breeze was springing up. Something warm and wet hit the back of my neck.

'Let's go on a boat!' Bel suggested, suddenly, excitedly.

Around us, plastic raincoats and parkas were being tugged out of bags. Through the crowds and the parked cars and the trellis of leaves, the shimmer of the lake turned slate-grey. Comforted by chips, eased by the car ride closer to goodness-knows-where, transported from the ghost town, I felt more relaxed, almost in a holiday mood. Rain reminds me of holidays – rain, and the smell of wet clothes, the squelch of water in plastic sandals, the steam of hair drying in a warm cafe, the sea pitted like orange skin, damp sandwiches, and someone saying, 'Why don't we ignore the rain and . . .'

'Right!' I smiled. 'Let's go on a boat.'

I had to be crazy. I slung my haversack on my back and helped Bel with the correct body-hug to use on her exploding bag. Then together, lumpily, we ran through the crackling rain, across the steamy pavements towards the jetty. The queue had disappeared into cars, shelters, chip shops and amusement arcades. There were just two goatherds waiting for the boat, kitted out in identical orange parkas and jaw-breaking smiles. And a tall blond boy in a sodden sweatshirt. He turned as we approached.

'Gawd!' Bel snarled. 'Guess what? The US Marines arrived ahead of us. Man the lifeboats.'

I smiled a sickly smile towards Michael O'Connor. He smiled nervously back. Bel ignored the attempt at transatlantic treaties, and stormed on.

'I'd accuse you of following us, but it's quite obvious that you're not. You're pushing in in front of us. Don't your lot know about "ladies first", and queuing up, and pearls before swine? You nicked our lift in the XJ6, Mickey Mouse, so don't try to grin your way out of it with your perfectly straightened teeth . . .' she raved.

'Um, how much is the boat-trip?' I asked, loudly and slowly, trying to show him that I didn't want to be involved in Bel's outburst, and trying to show her that enough was enough for one rainy day.

'Five pounds return,' he complained, gently. 'Too much for me. I'll have to take a rain-check.' I smiled at his quiet joke.

'A fiver! A fiver!' Bel shrieked.

I nudged her.

'I could live for a week on a fiver,' I whispered, reminding her.

'Or travel to Scotland,' she giggled. 'Sod the boat-trip. It's specially overpriced for pushy American tourists, anyway, and for orange aliens!'

I linked her arm and pulled her away, quickly, before the orange aliens came in for the attack. Michael had probably had enough of it, too.

It was only when we were on the main street,

walking towards Ambleside, sharing my anorak and thumbing desperately for lifts, that I realized I hadn't said goodbye to the American, and wondered whether it might have looked a little strange that we ran away again as soon as we saw him. I hoped he hadn't taken offence. But he looked too well-mannered to take offence, too chiselled for Bel's rudeness to do more than chip a little from his ego. Terry, now . . . Terry would have yelled after us, 'Hey, youse! Don't look now but your ignorance is showing!'

Chapter Seven

The rain changed everything. Of course, at first, it was as much of a joke as Bel could make it. She dragged me into a hardware shop on the edge of the town, where she bought dustbin bags, one to make into an instant raincoat, others to push the collapsing sausage bag into. She slung the sack over her shoulder like an incongruous Mother Christmas, and dived out of the shop again, to totter between raindrops and thumb lifts from pushbikes and from crocodiles of earnest hikers in fluorescent macs. The rain was warm, despite its persistence, and blue-grey, grey-green, as it spattered through leaves and across the surface of deserted lakes and tarns. Bel played Charlie Chaplin, danced, emptied rain from her shoes, made me join in with a frantic rendition of 'Singing in the Rain', and swung her sack defiantly.

But no one stopped for us. Cars piled with sodden holidaymakers aquaplaned past us, drenching us with the spray from racing wheels, the drivers tense and hunched behind clicking windscreen wipers. As the skies darkened and headlights peered through the foggy twilight under dripping tunnels of trees, Bel's spirits began to sag.

Mine, too. Huddled inside my waterproof, I was protected, and my feet were warm, dry and comfortable. I'd brought hiking boots and thick thermal socks. But, as the lights and bustle of Windermere gave way to the bleakness of bare fells and muddy wooded valleys, Bel's despondency reached out to me. It was as if both of us were moving away from everything we valued, and into a landscape in which we were nervous intruders, uncertain of our relationship with the world and with each other. We walked in silence to the beat of the rain, making for somewhere or other. There were no lights on the horizon, no lights behind us, and I realized that we'd both had enough. Bel's Worzel Gummidge appearance was doing nothing for our chances of getting a lift.

'Let's camp for the night,' I suggested in the end.

Bel was too tired and wet to argue. We headed into the darkness of trees, over wire, away from the main road, me leading, Bel cursing her shoes and holding on to my haversack for guidance. Eventually I found a level patch of ground in a damp cave of overhanging trees, and slung my haversack down. Somewhere among its contents were the instructions I'd cut out of a newspaper on how to make a bender, a waterproof igloo, from bent twigs, stone, and polythene sheeting. I had the polythene sheeting. I spread spare dustbin bags, retrieved from Bel's sack, on the ground, and went off in search of branches large enough to bend into shape.

Really, I needed Bel's help, but the sparkle wasn't there. She sat hunched and shivering on the bags, while I struggled to build a shelter. Like an automaton, she reacted when I asked her to hold one of the branches down, or tie it up, pass the string I'd brought or anchor something with a rock I'd collected.

'What's it supposed to be? Don't we ever get to the point where you say, "And here's one I made earlier," and produce something that looks totally professional? Meg – what the hell is it?' she shivered once with some of her old critical fire.

'It's a bender. Nuclear protesters live in them outside missile bases. It showed you how to make one in the paper the other day,' I explained, carefully. 'It's not perfect, but . . .'

'Say that again,' Bel challenged.

When, finally, a misshapen plastic bubble was erected, she crawled, sniffing, inside it and sat shivering under my thermal blanket, still clothed in black plastic, and made no offer to help me collect bits of dry wood for a small fire. The fire was half-hearted. I opened a can of beans and set it in the centre of the reluctantly smouldering twigs to heat.

The rain eased and set up flurries of spattering on the leaves above us while we shared the lukewarm beans, the remains of the bread and the last of the mint-cake. Then Bel arranged her wet clothes like festoons from the twigs inside the igloo, and scrambled into others that were a little less damp.

'Have six Brownie points, and a gold star, Megan. Tawny Owl is really pleased with you, and might even make you a sixer next week. Keep up the good work!' she muttered, covering herself with my dry clothes and shivering into sleep.

I'd like to say that I glowed with pride, that I had a deep and fulfilling sense of achievement and survival against the odds, but it wasn't like that. I felt empty, and very sorry for myself. The self-pity wasn't anything to do with the fact that I'd had to do most of the building and the cooking – that didn't really matter. I knew that, all things being equal, if I'd been in Bel's position, wet and tired with the effort of clowning, she'd have done the same for me. The emptiness had more to do with my failures than smug self-righteousness and resentment over my organizational skills. It was about me, Megan. Freckled, red-haired, reforming and lonely, and about Bel, confidently herself, who never needed to be polite or creeping, never needed to write poems of love to long-forgotten holiday romances, never needed to start building dreams on impossibilities. I wondered about the American, just briefly. Would he have asked me, if we'd ever spoken, 'Who was your rude friend? I really liked her.' I sat awake, with my Brownie points, and my gold star, and the contents of my survival kit, which was all I knew of reassurance. It was a long night, and bitterly cold until the sun came up and my eyes, like Bel's, finally closed.

In the morning, we awoke to find the polythene tent collapsed on us. Bel was stroppier than ever. I was more exhausted than ever. She pulled at her damp clothes, now spread over our makeshift bed, pushed them into bags and aimed punches at the plastic skin we were wrapped in.

'Little Bel woke bright and early to find the sky had fallen in while she was asleep,' she lisped, cynically, in a sickly sweet storyteller's voice. 'Ants were running up her leggings, her stomach was rumbling, her mouth felt like something under a manhole cover, and both her feet had turned into blisters. "Don't worry," said her tiny chum, Megan, the Mersey fairy. "This is just the start of a wonderful adventure." '

'Shuttup!' I groaned, trying to find my sandals, sticky with the humidity inside the plastic tomb. There was a butter sun in the sky, burning through the tree-tops, and mist rising from the damp undergrowth.

'Little Bel couldn't help thinking about her

mummy and daddy, back home, safe and warm in Wonderland, and her handsome prince, Tel the Magnificent, who was probably sitting in his magic castle at that very moment, eating hot toast and fried-egg sarnies. Megan, the Mersey fairy, was starting to get right up her nose . . .'

'Aw, for Christ's sake, Bel, pack it in, will you?' I screamed, crawling through the flap of polythene into the outside world. I tugged on the branches that held the igloo in place, tore at string, kicked boulders out of the way furiously.

'So what's up with you?' Bel asked, all innocence.

'What d'you think's wrong with me? It's not just you who's suffering, you know! I'm not too happy about this trip either. And if you remember, it wasn't my idea. I'd like to clean my teeth, wash my face, have a nice cup of tea and eat fried-egg sarnies as well. Don't you think I miss home?'

'So let's go home,' Bel said quietly, her tousled head appearing from the collapsed igloo.

'Yeah. Right. Home! We'll give up. That'd suit you, wouldn't it? You're running out of money. You can't last out much longer. And I'd have to go running back with you, I suppose, to keep you company. So what's in it for me? More nights of sitting in that cellar bar listening to them all sniggering at us, and moaning, and going on about how we proved that no one can manage on the dole,' I spluttered.

'I don't think they can,' Bel sighed, emerging, stretching in the sunlight. 'I've been thinking about it. I think Terry's right. I'm going to tell him when we get back.'

'You're going to tell him? You're going to admit that he was right and we were wrong? 'Course, it won't take an inch out of you! He'll put his arm round you and tell you how he knew all along that you'd never make it, but what about me? He won't get at you, Bel. He never does, not really. No one does. He'll just keep having a go at me, slagging me off, making sarky comments, being his usual nasty self.'

'Well you ask for it!' Bel snapped. 'There's something wrong with you, Megan. It's not that you're ugly or anything, it's not that you're thick. It's the opposite. You're too jumpy, that's all. You put yourself down, all clever-clever, and then get narked when other people do the same. It's like you wear prickles all the time. You'll never make it with a bloke if you keep on the way you do. It's no wonder . . .'

'Yeah?'

'It's no wonder that the only lad who ever fancied you was a teeny from some dead-and-alive hole in the Frozen North.'

'I wondered when we'd get round to that,' I snarled, pulling hard at the polythene, tearing it in my fury. 'I thought we'd get round to the toy-boy jokes before too long. So what makes you so wonderful? You can't even be polite to that poor Yank we keep bumping into. Talk about my prickles? You've got poisonous spines. Just because you've got your handsome prince back home – Tel the Magnificent – honestly! Well, it was me he was after at first, if you remember. Me! Then you came slinking up, making come-and-get-me eyes at him. It was pretty easy to read what you were saying, Bel. Some of us like to be a little bit choosy about flashing the sexual favours around. And some of us, mentioning no names but just watch my eyes, act like scrubbers!'

'Let me tell you,' Bel screamed, grabbing her dustbin sack and throwing everything haphazardly into it, 'that there's nothing like that between me and Terry. Not in the way you mean, anyway. Scrubber, eh? Scrubber? Well, now I know exactly what you think of me, I'll just say goodbye, and how unpleasant it was to know you. You've got some real problems. If a fella smiled at you you'd think he was trying to lay you. Tell you what, take a look in a mirror next time you find one. It could tell you a whole lot of things about sexual favours and why it doesn't look as if you've got any to give, and why no one would want them even if you tried to phoney them up. Terry was right. He said you were a frozen carrot. I'm off home!'

She found her shoes, struggled into them, defiantly, and stamped away through the trees. I heard twigs snapping, leaves rustling angrily, the noises echoing more and more distantly. I couldn't move. I stood, frozen in time, a carrot holding the ripped polythene, tears coursing down my cheeks. I didn't mean to say all that. I didn't. Bel had been my best mate since primary school, and I liked her more than I liked anyone. I liked her style and her brashness, her stupidity and her sharpness. I liked her, and I hated her for being loved by everyone, but especially by Terry, although I hadn't meant to let that slip out. Now she knew how bitterly envious I really was. 'Frozen carrot,' he called me. And me willing to throw myself passionately in his direction any time he'd care to test my temperature. 'Frozen carrot.' I shivered. The cold was the cold of isolation.

I flopped on to the damp leaves, pulled the polythene into my arms and howled into it, crying for me, and for the stupid overdrive of my jealous tongue that had driven even Bel away. I didn't know what I was going to do, now. There was no point in travelling on alone when I wasn't proving anything to anyone. But I couldn't go back, either, to face the mob in the cellar and Bel's lazy giggles. I couldn't.

There was a rustle of leaves. I looked up,

blinking, and Bel was standing there, hugging her dustbin sack, her shoes, one with a broken heel, hanging from one hand.

'Sorry,' she whispered.

'Me, too,' I said.

'I didn't mean any of those things I said, and they weren't true, anyway.'

'Same here.'

'I'm just knackered. Little Bel's done in. But I'm not giving up, just yet. We've got to go on, haven't we, kiddo?' she smiled, questioningly. 'Let's forget all that crap. Let's pretend we've just woken up in Wonderland and this is the start of a brand-new day.'

'Hitch to Penrith and Carlisle?' I asked.

'You're the boss. Anything you say,' she sighed, trying to smile.

Chapter Eight

Miracles can happen. Bel and I, dirty, tight-lipped and threatening-looking, burdened by dustbin bags and haversack, were picked up by the first car to come along the road that morning. It was a sunshine-yellow Beetle, a smiling sort of car that lifted our spirits even before the brakes were slammed on and the young driver shouted, 'Going as far as Penrith. Will that help?' Help? It was like divine intervention. One more hopeless hour of hitching would have decided me to give up to what I knew was now Bel's secret longing, to get back home as quickly as possible. She was on the brink of packing it all in, despite her offer to go on.

That couple saved us. They were young dental students, going to stay with her mum in Penrith. We told them about our bet, and the stupidity, but neither of them thought it was stupid, especially when Bel entertained them with exaggerated stories about racial warfare in Haverigg and the pushy American, the bread-van ride and the night in the forest. She didn't tell them about our row. We were both trying very hard, the scrubber and the frozen carrot, to pretend it had never happened. I was glad Bel found it so easy to jabber on. My stomach was gurgling and each time there was a dramatic pause in her recital, her stomach rumbled, too. Nick and Jess must have heard orchestral rumblings as well. Without warning, Nick pulled into a roadside cafe.

'Breakfast!' he announced. 'We'll buy you both breakfast.'

'Oh no, really. We couldn't,' I protested, very feebly.

'Yes, we could,' Bel nudged me. 'Terry said we could beg, con or steal. This is better than conning or stealing. And we haven't eaten since those cold beans last night. Thanks very much.'

They thought Bel was a riot. I suppose they thought breakfast was a small price to pay for a riot in a Beetle, especially as Nick was obviously trying to delay the meeting with Jess's mum. So, we were forced out of the car. Not that Bel needed a great deal of forcing. She was off and running towards the smell of bacon before I'd even found my towel and toilet bag. It seemed like a good opportunity to try to freshen up, as Nick suggested.

And well he might. In the mirror in the Ladies I was unrecognizable even to me. My hair was twined with grass and twigs and my face was smoky, apart from the pale tracks left by my tears.

'Is that me?' I howled to Bel.

'I'm not sure. Why don't you ask it?' she suggested.

Since we were the only customers in the cafe, the washroom was ours. We spread towels on the floor, stripped and washed in the basins – feet, legs and hair as well as face, body and undies. We cleaned our teeth, squirted ourselves with every spray we had, dried our hair under the hand-drier, changed, and emerged half an hour later to find a small queue outside the Ladies, all tutting and muttering about people who didn't realize that public conveniences were for the convenience of the public, not for exclusive use, and certainly not for half an hour.

Breakfast had been ordered and was steaming on the table: rashers of crisp bacon, plump Cumberland sausage, double eggs, black pudding, fried bread and potato scones, fruit juice, hot toast, pots of tea. Bel and I ate like savages. I'd never been so hungry, nor so grateful, in my life, and when, at the end of the meal, Bel asked me for two ten-pence pieces to phone Terry, I hadn't the heart to argue with her. I was too happy, too tired.

We slept in the car while it climbed the hills to Penrith. Contented, like two sleepy cats, lolling on the dustbin bags with our heads on each other's shoulders, we saw nothing and heard nothing until Nick shook us gently awake.

'I've driven through Penrith and out the other side. This is the slip-road to the motorway. Carlisle's only twenty or so miles up there. Hope you get another lift soon,' he grinned at us, watching us stretch and yawn and try to pull ourselves together.

'Thanks again,' I murmured.

'Thanks,' Bel had the grace to say.

We waved at the sunshine car until it disappeared into the haze on the horizon. Then we sat, still half-asleep, on the prickly grass by the side of the road, hitching half-heartedly. Despite the previous night's rain, the heat was oppressive, sullen and sticky. Clouds hung like dirty washing over the mountains.

'How much've we got left?' Bel asked, chewing a piece of dried-up grass.

'Six pounds twelve pence,' I told her, counting the change in my purse. 'That's altogether. But really, about four pounds of that's mine, and two is yours. I'll make it to John o'Groats. You might reach Carlisle.'

'And get back? See, there's that, isn't there? I thought about that last night while I was lying in the oxygen tent in the rain. I've gone past the point of no return. How do I get back from here on two pounds?'

I shrugged.

'We haven't tried conning or stealing, yet,' I said, trying to make a joke out of it. But the thought had occurred, sickeningly, to me, earlier in the day. Underneath, I was just as panic-stricken as Bel. It was just that I hadn't as much to pull me home.

'Think we'll make it?' she asked.

' 'Course we will,' I said. 'All we need is another couple of lifts like that one. We'll be in Scotland tonight, camp out for one more night, turn round and come back.'

'Speaking of lifts . . .' Bel said.

There was a squeal of brakes ahead of us. We both looked up. A blue van had pulled into the kerb, and the driver was yelling out of the passenger door, 'Do you two want a lift?'

Bel struggled to her feet, reflexively, started to fit her feet back into her second-best pair of crippling high heels, and pick up her bag. I put my hand on her arm, warningly. For some reason I felt uncertain about this one. The van was listing to one side. So was the driver. He had the face and teeth of a ferret and wore a grubby T-shirt. His face leered.

'Where are you headed?' I shouted to him.

'Where do you want to go?' he yelled back.

'It's not on,' I whispered to Bel who was trying to shrug my hand away. 'That proves it.'

'Proves what?' she argued, stepping towards the van.

'He's on the pick-up. He's not going anywhere in particular. He's just offering his services.'

'So? We can offer him a clip round the ear, can't we, if he tries anything on?' she whispered.

'Risky.'

'Carlisle?' she shouted at the ferret.

'You're on! But jump in before the battery goes flat!' he screamed at us. Before I could argue again, or quote my sixth sense at her, Bel had grabbed my hand and my rucksack and pulled and pushed me into the van.

'Carlisle it is!' the ferret said, grinning through his spiky teeth.

I didn't like him. I didn't trust him. I was squashed up next to him while Bel was pressed up against the door. I moved as far away from him as I could manage, ignoring Bel's grunts of protest, and watched his hand on the gear lever. It was one of those small, heavily knuckled, hairy hands with chewed nails and ingrained engine grease. His hair seemed to have been sculpted from the same grease. His bottom lip was full, and his prominent chin dark with heavy stubble. His T-shirt said Torremolinos University.

'Music?' he leered, switching on the cassette player which hung on a bracket below the cluttered dashboard. There were greasy rags, spanners, tyre wrenches and empty beer tins on the floor, spilling out of the open glove compartment. The small cab filled with the dull, heavy ache of country and western.

'Nice!' Bel sneered, raising her eyebrows at me. She still thought this was one big joke, someone to laugh at and make fun of for an hour or two. I wasn't so sure. I kept my eyes firmly on him, and on the little hairy hand. But, despite my good intentions, my eyelids started to droop, and my head lolled back on Bel's shoulder.

I awoke to a thumping on the partition behind me. Startled, my eyes blinked open. It was dark, but the darkness wasn't the darkness of night. We were lumbering through a tunnel of trees, and above us were storm clouds, purple-edged.

'Whaat . . .?' I stammered.

Bel jerked awake, too. The hairy hand patted my knee.

'No problem!' the ferret grinned. 'That's Johnno. He's been sleeping off his dinner in the back of the van. Open that hatch behind you, will you? Hey, Johnno, look what we've got here!'

Bel and I opened the hatch a fraction of an inch and peered through. There was a gorilla in the back of the van. It was pretending to be a human being, but nothing quite so big and hairy could hope to get away with it.

'Girls!' Johnno leered.

Bel closed the hatch on him, quickly.

'Let us out!' she yelled.

'What? Here? Don't be daft. We've come off the motorway down this short-cut. It's the middle of nowhere here . . .'

'Exactly!' Bel screeched.

'Let us out. Now!' I shouted, grabbing the hand that had wandered on to my knee and thrusting the little finger as far back as it would go. The van slithered and swerved. The ferret screamed.

'Now!' Bel shouted again. My hand reached across for the ignition keys. Ferret stamped on the brakes. The van struggled to stay upright and came to a juddering halt with its front wheels inches from the trunk of a towering oak tree. The ferret's head made contact with the windscreen. He reeled dazedly. I pulled out the screaming device from my jeans' pocket, pulled the chord until it emitted a dreadful high-pitched wail, shoved it in the glove compartment and locked it with the keys. Thunder sounded from the back of the van. Real thunder echoed it from the skies. The scream sounded out, louder than the thundering, into the darkness.

'No need to be unfriendly, girls!' ferret slurred, coming to. 'Switch that noise off. Someone'll think something's going on in here.'

'What's going on?' the gorilla howled from the back.

Bel opened the door and slid out. I pushed the dustbin bag after her, then my haversack, then dropped beside her, the ignition keys still in my hand. Flat, hot spots of rain splattered on to the road. As we started running, I threw the keys as hard and as far as I could and saw them land in a distant clump of thick undergrowth.

We stumbled along, through the rain. I turned round once and saw that the ferret had staggered out of the van and was searching hopelessly for his keys. We giggled at the shouts and yells and the rocking in the back of the van. And the scream.

'It shouldn't happen,' Bel said, suddenly, stopping dead.

'What shouldn't?'

'That sort of thing. Blokes and girls. Them grabbing all the time, us shoving them off. It's the system, see? You need a fella to keep the other fellas off you. Is that right?'

'Right and wrong,' I said, pushing her on. 'Right, it does happen. Wrong, because it shouldn't. But we looked after ourselves, didn't we? We survived.'

'I don't want to have to survive. I want to be comfy, like with Terry. If another bloke so much as looked at me, he'd stick one on him, and I wouldn't even have to think about the next move,' she whined.

'Right. You wouldn't have to think. You don't think when you're with him. It's just, "Yes, Terry, no, Terry, that guy's looking at me, Terry, hit him for me, Terry," ' I mocked in a little-girl voice. 'And that's you, Bel. The hard case that talked your way through the bikers. When you're with Terry, you turn into a shadow.'

'I love him, that's all,' she shrugged. 'And let me tell you something, that helpless act's a lot easier than putting on the tough act we're putting on now – God, doesn't that alarm ever stop screaming? Being helpless is sort of warm and cuddly, and it attracts the blokes. You ought to try it some time.'

'What, and lose out on all this?' I laughed, spreading my hands out to the lowering skies, the bare fells, the trees in the valley, the distant speck of a contorting blue van.

'Yeah . . . all this!' she laughed, too, whooping with hysteria. I tried to hold her up, and hold myself up, but I was laughing too hard as well. We wiped our eyes, and then started laughing again, before Bel drew breath and pointed towards a main road ahead of us. 'Carlisle 5 miles' a huge sign read.

'Civilization this way!' she shouted.

'Oh no . . .' I breathed.

Ahead of us, standing hitching on the main road, was Michael O'Connor. Bel saw him, too. And we both saw the car. It was coming to a dignified halt a little in front of the American, a little closer to us.

'This time, let's strike a blow for equality. Let's do it to him, before he does it to us again,' Bel screamed.

Distracted by her shout, Michael O'Connor looked towards us, instead of at the car.

'Run!' Bel yelled, over her shoulder, diving towards the door of the car. 'For Gawd's sake, run, Megan, will you?'

And then she seemed to buckle, like a hinge, and keeled over.

'Bel! Bel!' I cried, running now, my haversack

tearing at my shoulders. Michael seemed to be running, too, towards us both, towards the car.

'Get in!' Bel screamed. 'Get me in. I've done my ankle in. I can't move!'

I anchored my hands under her armpits and tried to lift her into the car. The elderly couple in the front seats looked at each other, warily, scared obviously by the chaos that their small act of kindness had created.

'Here. Let me,' Michael called, kneeling down and picking Bel up, almost effortlessly. 'Second time you've fallen for me, huh?'

'My ankle!' Bel howled.

'Is there room for all three of us?' Michael asked.

The woman in the passenger seat nodded, mystified. Michael lifted Bel carefully into the car and nodded to me to follow.

'Carlisle?' I asked.

'That's where we're going,' the driver admitted.

'Would it be possible for you to drop us at the hospital?' Michael asked, concern deepening his voice.

'Bel?' I asked, shakily.

'It's my ankle . . .' she sobbed.

'OK, OK, we'll get you to a hospital,' I stammered, shutting the car door behind me.

Chapter Nine

The dream was over. That much was obvious even before Bel's ankle was put under medical scrutiny. She was enclosed inside the flowery curtains of a cubicle in Outpatients, deep in serious discussion with a snub-nosed nurse, and we were sitting, the American and I, waiting on damp canvas chairs, dripping on to our piled haversacks. It felt like the end. It smelt like the end: synthetic pine disinfectant, anaesthetic and stewed tea, wet clothes and sweaty palms. For days that seemed like weeks, stretching out from cold dawns to clammy sunsets, we'd kept ourselves to ourselves, isolated from crowds, in the quiet company of trees and birds, in the shadows of mountains. Now, people intruded, watched us with sick furtive eyes, coughed, cried gently to themselves, squealed from cubicles, or rattled WVS teacups. I watched Michael, but didn't know what to say. For some reason he looked at home, unruffled, interested in what was going on around us, but frowning, as if he had his own problem to contend with.

The frown made his face more interesting, somehow. It puckered his forehead, bushed out his eyebrows, made his mouth look less perfect, more pensive. His eyes, too, now that they were clouded, were a deeper, harsher blue. It wasn't too much of a lived-in face, not like Terry's, but it had a life of its own, not something borrowed from male models in teen-magazines, or the bland disinterestedness of faces in American sit-coms. It was no longer the kind of face I expected an American to have. I smiled nervously at him when he caught me scrutinizing him. I blushed. He smiled back, almost as nervously. All right, so I knew it was Bel that he liked. I'd seen the careful, concerned way he'd picked her up, the gentle way he'd tried to calm her when she was doing one of her over-the-top hysterical monologues on the way to the hospital. I'd seen the way he touched her ankle, with a tenderness that clenched me with jealousy again. But so what if he fancied Bel? I could like him, couldn't I? I could just like his frowning face and his little smile. I was allowed to do that much. But I didn't want to push any harder than that.

'It's OK,' I sniffed. 'You don't have to hang around. We can manage.'

'No problem. I'm inside my schedule for today. Carlisle's my target, and I'm already here. Anyway, I'd like to see what's wrong with your friend, OK?' he asked.

'OK,' I shrugged. He sounded quite kind and interested. And there was something else, too . . .

He cleared his throat.

'Something I figure I should tell you,' he croaked, quietly. He cleared his throat again. 'I may be wrong, it's possible, but I reckon there's nothing wrong with your friend's ankle.'

'What!' I breathed.

'It could just be a simple sprain, but I doubt even that. There was no swelling, no bruising, the bone was intact. Would there be any reason for her to fake a twisted ankle?'

'No . . . no . . . she wouldn't do that!' I

whispered, almost to myself. 'Not even Bel. She wouldn't go that far.'

But perhaps she would. All day I'd been pushing her beyond her limits. Until the rain, she'd been enjoying the adventure, willing to put her own brand of initiative into everything we'd tried to do. But there'd been subtle warnings. There'd been that phone call to Terry from the cafe, for instance. There'd been the outburst of homesickness and lovesickness after we'd escaped from the van. There'd been her real reluctance, since morning, to carry on, despite her sudden reappearance after her dramatic exit from the forest. Could Bel do a thing like that, though? Pretend to have a broken ankle and lose the bet for both of us? No, even for her that was going too far. The suggestion was ludicrous, and insulting.

'Anyway, what do you know about it?' I snarled at Michael, hot in defence, now, of my best friend against this stranger, this foreigner.

'I'm a medical student,' he said, quietly.

'So?' I blustered, trying to cover up my surprise at this sudden display of expertise. 'So what do medical students know? I bet you never got down as far as ankles on your course, yet. I bet you've only just learned how to wear a stethoscope and how to iron a white coat!'

'Right!' he laughed, surprisingly, and almost cynically. 'You're right. But I come from a long line of doctors. My father's a Navy surgeon, and my mother was a nursing sister. My brother, Patrick,' his voice trailed off a little and lost itself before he finished lamely, '. . . is a medical student, too. At Johns Hopkins. That's a good school. The best.'

'Is that where you are?' I asked.

'No. I never was the best,' he said.

'So what makes you think you're right about my

mate?' I snapped, although a bit surprised by his honesty.

'OK. You want me to go?' he said, softly, picking up his haversack.

'No . . . no . . . please. Listen. I'm sorry. I'm on edge. It's just that this trip means so much to me. It's a bet, see. Someone's bet us that we can't reach Scotland on five pounds . . .'

His forehead furrowed again. I put a restraining hand on his. He dropped his haversack and raised his eyebrows, questioningly.

Exhaustedly, I explained to him about the bet, mentioning no names, mentioning none of the emotional background and blackmail that had led to my acceptance of the bet.

'Less than ten dollars!' Michael whistled, when I'd finished outlining the terms of the bet.

'See? Not easy, eh? The guy who made the bet with us has this theory that you can't live like a human being on unemployment money.'

'Neat theory.'

'But if Bel can't, or won't, go on, we can't prove anything, can we? And we're so close . . . so close . . .' I murmured.

A hand tapped me on the shoulder. It was the snub-nosed nurse from Bel's cubicle.

'Your mate wants to talk to you,' she said, in a thick Scouse accent.

'You're from the 'Pool,' I breathed.

'Yeah. That's what she wants to talk to you about,' the nurse said, winking.

I didn't quite understand, but I followed her to the cubicle, anyway. Bel wasn't lying, crippled in pain, on the bed, but sitting on a chair, swinging her legs. Her feet were still squashed into her impossible shoes.

'Don't say it . . .' she pleaded.

'You've been skiving! You conned me – and him! There's nothing wrong with your ankle!' I gaped.

'Right. Karen said I should own up. Oh, by the way, this is Karen,' she said, pointing to the nurse who had followed me in. 'Anyway, Karen said there's no way she's taking me to X-ray, because she sussed me out, straight off, didn't you, Karen? So this is the truth, Meg. I just wanted to get that lift before the Yank, and a busted ankle was the only way I could think of doing it. Stop gawping at me like that, because it worked, didn't it? We got the lift, and we got more than that! Just listen – Karen's got the weekend off. She's driving straight back to her mum's in Liverpool and, wait for it, she's offered us both a lift home!'

'Um . . . after we've been to Scotland?' I asked, dumbstruck.

'No, dimmo. Now! In half an hour, to be exact. We're on our way back, no charge! And she'll even call in at Aunty Esme's so I can pick up the rest of my gear and get my case. How about that!'

'No. I don't want to turn back now,' I said, numbly but definitely.

'It's for the best, Meg. I miss Terry. I miss him, like there's no tomorrow. Come on. Do your best mate a favour. Let's get back,' she wheedled, putting her arm round me.

'No, Bel. No!' I shouted. The anger surprised even me. I'd always thought I kept my feelings under control.

'Well, please yourself!' she announced, totally unmoved by my fury. 'I'm off. Go on alone if you want to. But I'm off.'

I stormed from the cubicle and over to the chair where I'd been sitting.

'Congratulations, doctor,' I sniffed. 'Looks like

you were spot on with your diagnosis. The nurse offered us both a lift back to Liverpool, in half an hour's time. So, that's it.'

'You're giving up?' Michael asked, bewildered.

'So tell me, what option do I have? I can't go on alone. There'd be no point, and I couldn't manage anyway. I'll just have to do what she wants,' I shouted exasperatedly.

'Not necessarily,' Michael said, thoughtfully.

'What d'you mean, not necessarily? What d'you mean? The whole thing's off!' I howled.

'I could take Bel's place,' he murmured.

'What?'

'I could be her, to all intents and purposes.'

'You'd look silly in those shoes!' I shrieked, disbelief forcing me into a pointless funny.

'Apart from the dress-sense, I could do it. Stand in for her, take her share of the money. I could use my own money to stock us up with more food for the rest of the journey to Scotland. It's not far. We could go on together,' he smiled.

'You and me?' I breathed.

'Why not?' he asked. 'I'm making for Scotland, anyway. This wouldn't take me off my itinerary.'

'Fantastic!' I shouted, throwing my arms round him, kissing his salty neck. One of the outpatients whistled. Someone clapped. I realized what I'd done, and stepped back, dropping my arms in amazement.

Michael O'Connor looked equally embarrassed.

'Hadn't I better try those shoes on?' he grinned, twinkling shyly.

I could hardly believe it. I raced back to the cubicle, to Bel who was repacking her dustbin bag, and Karen, who was trying to negotiate for me, and hugged both of them as well. Excitedly, I explained what had happened, and the deal Michael O'Connor was offering.

'Hmm,' Bel murmured.

'Meaning?'

'I reckon you've struck lucky there. Could be that he fancies you.'

'Don't be daft!' I argued.

'You couldn't make it tonight, though,' Karen said, looking at her watch. 'It's half-seven already. Hitching in the dark's too difficult round here. Tell you what, why don't you camp out in my flat tonight? You could take my key and leave it with Rosie, next door, in the morning. You could eat up any rubbish I've left in the fridge. You'd be doing me a favour, actually. I don't like leaving the place empty. It's a rough area.'

'How about that, then!' Bel whooped. 'I hope you'll thank me for this in years to come. Remember, if I hadn't copped out, you wouldn't have had your chance at this great night of intimacy and passion with the blond bombshell.'

'Shut up, Bel!' I squirmed, blushing deeply. Her suggestiveness was painful. So was Karen's suggestion. I didn't fancy being holed up, all night, in someone's flat, with a stranger. I wouldn't know what to do, or to say.

'I'll discuss it with the American,' Karen decided.

I felt as if my future was being taken out of my hands. I was certain that Michael O'Connor would react with the same horror to the suggestion that we stay in Karen's flat as I had. He seemed to be just as pernickety and as nervous as I was. I tried to think of alternatives. He could stay in a youth hostel tonight. I could stay in Karen's flat alone. But, if it was a rough area, would I feel safe?

'All sorted out,' Karen said, coming back into the

cubicle. 'He thinks it's a great idea. So let's get everyone organized. I'm now officially off duty. Collect your bags and let's go.'

I felt like a new robot, stiff all over with the indignity of having been invented by someone else. Michael and I hardly looked at each other on the walk to the car park, and hardly spoke in the car. Bel didn't speak much either, but she nudged me raw, and winked at me so regularly that she looked as if she had a nervous twitch. We were shown into a neat compact flat in a Victorian three-storey house at the edge of town. Karen showed us around, collected her case, and then handed the key over to Michael.

'Make yourselves at home,' she smiled, as if it was the most natural thing in the world. Bel just kept winking.

'I'll tell Terry you're making it!' she whispered on the way out.

'Don't you dare!'

'The trip to Scotland, I mean,' she said, all innocently.

Then the door closed behind them, and Michael O'Connor and I stood looking at each other warily.

Chapter Ten

I saw an old movie, once, in which an unmarried couple had to share a room for the night. They divided the room with a sheet strung across a clothes-line. If Michael and I had found a clothes-line, I think we would have done the same thing. As it was, we stalked the territory, nervously, checking out for a second time where everything was. Then he threw his haversack on to the sofa.

'I'll sleep here,' he said. 'You take the bedroom.'

'OK,' I agreed mildly.

'And can you cook?'

'I can cook up excuses for not being able to cook,' I said.

'That sounds rehearsed.'

'I've said it before,' I admitted.

'Just as well I can cook, then,' he grinned. 'Let's see what we've got here . . .' He opened the fridge in the cooking end of the living-room and pulled out a tray of eggs and some bacon. Eggs and bacon, I thought.

'No problem. Omelettes,' he said. 'There's some wilting lettuce, too, and a spring onion, and a tomato, so we can have salad. Why don't you take a bath?'

'That bad, is it?' I asked, sniffing.

'Just so you can't check out how bad *I* am at cooking. Go on!' he laughed.

I was grateful for the release. In Karen's bright

bedroom, with its framed posters, rainbow curtains and unmade bed, I took out my cleanest pair of trousers and a loose top I hadn't worn yet. Everything else was smelly, the kind of smell that attaches itself to clothes that have been damp and haven't dried out properly. I took them with me into the bathroom, soaked for as long as I could in the steamy warmth of the bath, then dumped all my clothes into the grubby water and stamped on them, singing tunelessly, nervous and happy at the same time, thankful for the rest, the comfort and the warmth, and for the smells creeping under the door. Food.

Why had I pretended I couldn't cook? Probably because I didn't dare cook for him. I didn't know what Americans ate, or what he ate. He would have stood over me, watching, and I'd've been all fingers and thumbs, trying to make an impression and messing everything up. So, instead, I beat and stamped hell out of my dirty clothes, squeezed them tightly and hung them to dry on the line across the bath.

'What kept you?' he asked when I finally emerged, and placed a perfect omelette down in front of me at the table he'd set with mats and a single unlit candle.

'Washed my clothes,' I explained. Then, as an afterthought, 'D'you want me to do any washing for you? Socks?'

'That bad, is it?' he asked, laughing.

I liked that. In all the awkwardness between us and the difficult position we'd been placed in, he could still remember what I'd said and quote me back at myself. It was a game only friends played, usually, and Michael O'Connor couldn't really be a friend. He was too old, too different.

'How old are you?' I asked, between mouthfuls of

an omelette that was so perfect, so golden, that, chauvinistically, I couldn't understand how a mere male could have made it.

'Nineteen last month,' he said. 'And you?'

'Seventeen next year,' I said.

'That's about what I figured,' he said.

The conversation had awkward gaps. In the gaps we ate, smiled, tried to look reassuringly at each other and were over-polite in passing the salad and bread. Sometimes we started to say something together, and there was that silly business of 'Sorry,' 'You were saying?' 'No, you first,' 'No, go on,' which just made the trivial thing each of us was mumbling sound even more trivial. Then, over coffee, I told him about Liverpool, about Bel, about the journey so far. I mentioned, just the once, a boyfriend. I called him Terry. Well, why not? I didn't know whether I was being self-protective or making myself sound more interesting with that fib. He told me about living in Washington at the Naval base, about his 'hick' college and his brother Patrick. He said a great deal about his brother. He told me about the trip they'd taken together, the year before, to Ireland, and how he'd decided to come to what he called the UK this year, on his own. I listened to most of what he was saying, but little really penetrated. It was that anxious listening, where you're just trying to take hold of hints and clues to the other person's life-style and personality.

Michael O'Connor, I decided before I'd finished my coffee, was a strange sort of boy. For an American, he seemed to be short on confidence, too thoughtful for his own good. I didn't like the anxious way he described his father. And I didn't like the way he referred, more than once, to a girl called Sandie. So much for Bel's idea that he fancied me. Sandie was slotted into the conversation at the wrong times, and in the wrong contexts, as if she was on his mind but not easy on his mind. And then there was Patrick. Over and over again, there was Patrick.

'Great omelette,' I said, at the end of the meal, when I stacked the dishes and took them to the sink to wash up.

'Patrick's recipe,' he said. 'He showed me, years ago, how to make omelettes. You never forget anything Patrick teaches you.'

'This bloke sounds more like your patron saint than your brother,' I grinned, in a sarky, throw-away manner, over my shoulder, from the sink.

But the comment had a strange effect. He stiffened, bristled almost, muttered something about having to wash his socks, and disappeared into the bathroom. After that, there was no more conversation. We nodded and smiled good-nights, and went separately to our sides of the sheet on the clothes-line, he to the sofa, I to the cosiness of the unmade bed.

I slept like a log, untroubled by any further questioning or analysis of the life and times of Michael O'Connor. Although the day had been punctuated by snatched-at sleep, in Nick's car and in the ferret's van, it had been a day of storms, one way and another, and the exhaustion of the last few days had finally caught up with me. The night of passion that Bel had winkingly predicted was a night of dreamless sleep, until the moment I lurched awake, sensing an intruder in my room.

For a moment or two, I couldn't get my bearings. The rainbow curtains, suffused with soft morning light, were frighteningly unfamiliar. The posters on the wall, bookshelves, the voice of someone who wasn't Mum holding out a cup of tea to me, scared me so much I almost cried out.

'Six a.m.,' Michael whispered, obviously almost as startled as I was. I'm rarely a pretty picture in the morning, particularly at six o'clock, a time I'm not usually familiar with.

'Six?' I screamed, hoarsely. 'Six?'

'Time to eat breakfast and to make a move, if we want to get on the road and get you to Scotland,' he murmured.

When I'd settled myself again, gulped the tea, visited the bathroom, breakfast was laid out on the table, as efficiently as dinner had been. Glasses of orange juice gleamed on the table like sunlight. He'd made toast, too, and a jug of coffee. Nice guy. And a nice smile. Shame about the girlfriend. I sat opposite him, smiling stupidly to myself.

'So . . . I've plotted out my route. Correction. Our route. It's not very far at all,' he said, offering me the toast. 'We should be there late morning. Then I'll see you on to your road back home.'

I gulped into my orange juice.

'That *was* the deal, wasn't it?' he asked, frowning at my obvious surprise. 'You wanted to get over the border. Here . . .' he produced a map from his haversack, '. . . this is where the border is. I'll see you right with a decent lift back. It's easy when you know how. We'll look for a couple coming back from vacation in Scotland. I know all the best places to hitch-hike from – drive-ins and picnic-spots. OK?'

'I . . . I thought the deal was that you took Bel's place. For however long it takes for the money to start running out,' I stammered.

He shook his head. He looked certain about the part he had to play.

'Just over the border,' he insisted.

'Oh,' I whispered.

All the new hope and energy, the good night's

sleep, the morning sunshine, were dulled by this latest turn up for the books. Michael seemed unaware of my disappointment. He chomped toast, examined maps, obviously choosing where he was going to travel to, once he'd dumped me. I'd expected too much. True, I hadn't been led to expect anything more than what I was now being offered. It was just that I'd *thought* there was something more, a kind of companionship that would make him want to spend more time with me, as I'd begun to want to know him better and to spend some time with him until I had to return home to the boredom and the snide jokes, and Bel and Terry smooching in the corner of the cellar bar. I knew I'd be something of a heroine when I got back, especially now that Bel had returned and could tell stories about the romantic meeting I'd had along the way, with this stunning American, and about the romantic night I'd spent alone with him. I trusted Bel to embroider that story beautifully and present it, in all its exaggeration, to Terry, who might, just might, feel a pang of jealousy. But if I went home today, how could I explain what had happened? Terry would probably say that one night with me was obviously too much, even for a Yank. I needed to use Michael O'Connor to get back at Terry, didn't I? That was more than half the reason for my disappointment. The other fraction of the reason was the frown he was frowning, that uncertain look that made me want to run my fingers along the creases and puckers and say, 'Don't worry. Don't worry about a thing. Whatever it is, it'll be all right.'

'From what you said last night,' he said, breaking into my disappointment and rejection, 'it seemed clear to me that you were in a hurry to get back home to your boyfriend, once you've cleared the terms of the bet. Terry, I think you said his name was.'

'Ah . . .' I blushed.

'You miss him?' he asked, sharply.

I shrugged.

'Naturally,' I said.

But did I? Did I really remember more than a wicked gap-toothed smile, and the way it used to make me feel hot with cold edges? Terry, and the way I felt about him, never was much more than a desperate lie at the best of times, an excuse to make me feel I needed someone as much as Bel needed him. But all he really did was hurt my pride. I enjoyed the battle with him because it was exciting. Now it didn't seem quite so exciting, or so necessary.

'Like you miss Sandie,' I added.

'Well, that's . . .'

'Listen,' I murmured. 'I'm going to tell you the truth. I want to get as far as I can with the money I've got, not just over the border, but as far away from Terry Macdolan as possible. He's not my boyfriend. He's Bel's. And I've resented that for far too long.'

He put his toast down, and his map, suddenly attentive. So I told him the whole story, how I met Terry, how he fell for my best friend, and how I'd never got over it. I told him about my hidden envy of Bel, and the way it flared up from time to time even on our trip together. Michael listened, batting his sandy eyelashes, his eyes deeper blue than ever. They say that when you tell a deeply guarded secret you feel better about it, but not me. I felt ashamed, unburdening myself like that to a stranger.

'This trip has everything to do with Terry. He was the one who bet us we couldn't do it, and honestly, Michael . . .'

'Mike,' he corrected, absent-mindedly.

'Mike, he was betting me, not Bel. *He* knew, you see. He wants to make me suffer, because I've had this thing about him. He wants to put one over on me, and I want to put one over on him, too. Well, that's not a relationship, is it? It's . . . I don't know what it is . . .'

Michael shook his head.

'It's a kind of contest. It's something I know a whole lot about. You and me, we got more in common than you know.'

For a moment, a fleeting second, his hand rested on mine, just touching. Just enough. Then, 'Let's get it together,' he said, gruffly, collecting the plates. 'We'd better see how far away from him you can get.'

'You'll help?' I whispered.

'That's what I'm saying, isn't it? Come on, you got to clear your junk from the bathroom, and I got to do this washing up.'

'I'll do the washing up,' I volunteered, suddenly dizzy with relief and happiness. Perhaps it was a good thing, after all, to unburden myself to a stranger. Something had just started to unfold its sticky wings. Something could almost be about to take off.

Chapter Eleven

It was strange setting off from Karen's flat with Mike by my side instead of Bel. He wasn't as outrageous, explosive or unpredictable, he wasn't as giggly or as moody, but he felt like a friend, all the same, and he was a thousand times more efficient. We stopped at a supermarket, where he stocked up with bread, butter, cheese and ham, cereals and skimmed milk, fruit and chocolate. The amount he bought suggested that he was buying for two of us, and for more than just one day. He consulted me about most of what he bought. I'd been accepted. We were going to conquer Scotland together.

While we stood on the slip-road leading to the motorway, he discussed the route we'd take. He'd decided to see Glasgow, and the west coast, then travel inland and cross-country to Edinburgh and the east. It sounded a good plan. I didn't like it much.

'What's wrong with that?' he asked, when I registered no particular approval.

'It's a bit cut and dried, isn't it? Glasgow tomorrow, Edinburgh with a little luck by Thursday, taking in every historical monument and waving to the Loch Ness Monster on the way; working it all out with maps, and distances covered.'

'It's just the way we did it last year – well, the way Patrick did it. Forward planning, he called it.'

'Boring, I call it. Why not just close our eyes, cross our fingers, and see what happens?' I grinned.

'Well . . .' he considered.

Just after that, a car stopped for us. It was a hire car, with the sticker in the back window announcing that it had been rented in London. A woman with tight mouse curly hair and an owlish face peered out of the passenger window as we ran up.

'Hi,' she called. 'Saw the stars and stripes!'

Another American. She'd noticed the huge sticker on Michael's bag and seemed only too eager to find some home-from-home conversation in an alien land.

'Get in, get in. How far are you going?' she beamed.

'Scotland,' Mike and I chorused.

'We're only going as far as Stranraer, but you're more than welcome,' she said, helping to settle both of us, and our haversacks, in the back seat.

'This is Ricky,' she introduced us to her husband, who was balding, with glasses, open-neck T-shirt and smiling friendly face, 'and I'm Kay. We're from Vermont. We're doing the UK this year. Started three days ago, in London, and we're right on schedule. And you two, what part of the States are you from?'

'Washington DC,' Mike said.

'Liverpool UK,' I said.

'Liverpool? You're not American?' Kay asked, apparently surprised that the world contained people who weren't from the USA. 'We saw Liverpool, didn't we, Ricky? We saw the signs for it, off the motorway, but we didn't make the detour. Did you know the Beatles?'

'Not my generation,' I smiled. Mike raised his eyebrows at me, behind her back. She was obviously kind-hearted, but more the conventional American tourist than Mike. As we drove along the anonymous contours of the motorway, she interrupted her monologue from time to time to point out details of the surrounding landscape to Ricky, who just smiled, nodded, and concentrated on his driving.

'So what're you two doing, travelling together?' Kay asked.

I let Mike explain. He spoke the language. The idea of the bet obviously intrigued Kay. When the border signs flashed past the car, she led us all in a cheer to celebrate making our first objective. It made me feel good, knowing that I'd achieved what I set out to do, knowing that with Mike's help I could achieve more. But now that the critical point had been passed, the need for it had already disappeared. The journey was no longer a case of my proving something to a boy who wasn't really interested in me, anyway; it was now a kind of holiday, a journey into the future, something just for me. Terry didn't have any further part in it.

Kay and Ricky insisted on treating us to coffee at the first motorway service station. I bought a postcard for my mum and wrote 'Made it to Scotland' on it under Michael's close scrutiny. He picked it up and examined it before I posted it.

'So that's your address?' he asked. 'Here, let me write it in my little black book. I'll give you mine, later. Maybe we could, you know, write to each other when this is all over?'

'OK,' I said happily.

'And now we'd better ask this wonderful couple to drop us off at the next slip-road. If we go on to Stranraer with them, we'll be going out of our way,' he said, putting his pen and book away.

'Better keep to the schedule. No time for detours. That's what they said. It's what Patrick says, too, isn't it? Schedules. Forward planning,' I teased.

A muscle twitched in his cheek. Whenever I mentioned Patrick, there was the same closing up, the same tension. I had the feeling that Mike was under some kind of pressure from his older brother.

Ricky and Kay were waiting for us in the cafeteria, grumbling about English coffee until I reminded them that it was Scottish coffee, and bubbling over about some secret plan they'd obviously been discussing. Kay was bubbling over. Ricky looked as if he never got beyond the point of slow simmer.

'I just been talking to Ricky, and we've come up with something you're just gonna love!' Kay squealed, grabbing one of my hands and one of Mike's. 'See, we're not going just to Stranraer. We're going to Ireland, on the ferry. Got the ticket prebooked for the night sailing. And Ricky and I think that we'd like to offer you the chance to come with us. No charge! We've just loved having your company, and crossing with four people in the car won't be a big surcharge. We've booked a cabin, but you could grab a nap on those reclining chairs, couldn't you? We get to Larne in the middle of the night, then we're driving across the country to do the Ring of Kerry. We could take you as far as that. Then you'll have one more country, and you'll get more points on your initiative test!'

'Two,' Mike corrected her. 'Northern Ireland and Eire.'

'It's not about points,' I said at the same time.

But the idea was good. It was exciting. I'd been on the ferries, but never on a boat as far as Ireland. To get across the sea would be something I'd be able to boast about to Bel.

'Let's do it!' I breathed.

'No,' Mike snapped, and then, more gently, 'There's Glasgow . . .'

'Forget Glasgow. Let's take this offer. I've always wanted to see Ireland, and you've been there, you can tell me about it. Please!'

'Yeah! Why not? Let's forget the forward planning and the schedules,' he enthused, suddenly.

'Thanks!' I bubbled to Kay. 'That's a great idea. Fantastic!'

'Thanks,' Mike smiled, as if he'd lost some weight he'd been carrying around. But, then, doubts set in a little. He sat quietly, staring out of the car window as the journey resumed.

It was settled. Kay was more excitable and chattery than ever for the rest of the journey to Stranraer, but I'd warmed to her. I even began pointing out things of interest to Ricky, and discussing some of the quainter aspects of British life with the two of them: soccer fanaticism, for instance, when a coach-load of screaming fans, scarves streaming from the windows, stormed past us. Ricky and Kay joined in with their review of American football and baseball. Mike, who had been thoughtful since the decision to go to Ireland had been reached, began to contribute, himself, to this conversation, and before long the three of them were trying to convince me of the finer points of their home teams. It wasn't much different from sitting in the cellar listening to Terry and his mates arguing over Liverpool and Everton. Once again, I felt like a referee.

The Scottish landscape slid past, green and violet, ribboned with streams, on a grander and bleaker scale than the Lake District, but none of them seemed interested. I was. It was so different from the flatlands of Liverpool and the cosy intimacy of city life. I wanted to get out and walk, climb a mountain, sit on a stone bridge over the stream, throw pebbles into the water, and dream a little. There wasn't much time in the efficient schedule the Americans had worked out for themselves. By the time Stranraer appeared on the horizon, Kay had thrown away all pretence of remembering where she was and needing to record it, as I was trying to do, on her mind. She had unearthed some photographs of the July 4th parade in her Vermont home town and was passing them to me in breathless wonder, pointing out the succession of decorated bicycles and floats. Mike and Ricky were discussing the relative merits of the Dodgers and the Rams. When we arrived in Stranraer we'd become friends, as well as adoptive lame ducks, and were herded into an hotel for a Scottish high tea.

Despite my reservations about accepting a free meal, as well as a free boat-trip, I was famished and only too happy to fill myself to overflowing with American generosity and hospitality. But Kay was exhausting. I fell, briefly, asleep while we sat in the car waiting our turn in the queue for the ferry, and was relieved when Kay directed us towards the lounge with the reclining chairs and disappeared into the cabin she and Ricky had booked. I almost fell into my seat, stretched out, and was asleep before the boat sailed. Mike lay on the seat next to me, his eyes open, staring at the ceiling. He'd disappeared inside himself again. I wanted to ask what was wrong. It was obviously something to do with Ireland, something that brought back memories that he didn't want to stir up, but I was too sleepy to say anything. Instead, I reached out and settled my hand on his, on the armrest between us. He smiled, quickly and sadly, at me before my dreams took over.

Chapter Twelve

I awoke in what seemed like the middle of the night. My stomach churned. There was a throbbing noise in the background, and the greasy smell of cooking. Someone was playing a radio. Kids cried. A drunk sang. The air was thick with stale smoke and the acidic smell of the nearby toilets.

'Mike!' I groaned, tapping him awake. 'I think I'm going to be sick.'

He blinked blearily at me, then seemed to realize where he was, and who I was. Something in my expression must have convinced him that I was making a fairly reasonable prediction about my state of health.

'Come on,' he murmured. 'We'd better get you on to the deck.'

'Oh God, what's happening?' I moaned, feeling the waves of nausea rising into my throat.

'The boat's moving, that's all. No problem,' he insisted, helping me up the swaying staircase to the deck.

'No problem!' I heaved. 'No problem?'

It was the first time I'd felt anything approaching seasickness. My head was full of things I wanted to forget – specifically tomato soup, gammon and pineapple and cauliflower cheese, fried potatoes, scones with jam and cream. I tried to shut the evening meal out of my mind, but still it expressed itself in no uncertain terms in my stomach. I was hot, sweaty, unable to focus.

'Fresh air,' Mike announced, dragging me on deck.

It was cold. That was a welcome relief. And dark. And almost deserted. Only a few stalwarts stood watching the lights of Larne on the approaching shore. The cold and the fresh salt breeze caught in my throat, easing the nausea almost immediately. I held on to the railing, looked out towards the lights and inky swelling sea, let the wind catch my hair and tangle it into tiny whips, but I felt better.

'See, I told you. It works every time. It's the stuffiness down there. It used to get to me, when my father tried to persuade me I was going to be a great sailor. We were stationed in West Germany and used to take trips across the North Sea to Harwich. Is that how you say it?' Mike asked. He pronounced it Hahrwitch. I corrected him.

'Patrick was fine. He was six, then, and I was just five. Patrick always had a strong stomach. But I was always ill. I looked like you looked a minute or two ago.'

'How was that?' I asked.

'Your face was kinda fluorescent,' he laughed. 'You looked like a kid dressed up for Trick or Treat. Sick!'

'How does it look now?' I asked, nervously.

'Coming back to life,' he grinned.

'So, you were posted in Europe, once?' I asked, going back to the previous conversation.

'Dad's been posted all over: Europe, Middle East, Far East. When we were kids, we used to be carted around all over the globe. It's easier now he's at

Bethesda. We're settled. Have been for six years.'

'And you don't fancy Navy life?'

'No way! Patrick does, though. He'll take his commission when he graduates from med. school. Me, I don't know. Don't know yet if I'm doing the right thing . . . but, no problem.'

'What d'you mean, no problem? It obviously is a problem. What's the matter? Are you in big brother's shadow, or something? Trying to be like him and not quite making it?' I asked, gently enough. At least, I thought the question was gentle. But Liverpool questions have this tendency to sound blunt and harsh.

'So what're you, suddenly? A social worker?' he snapped.

'That's what my mum is,' I stammered. 'Does it show? Listen, I'm sorry. I didn't mean to pry. If you don't want to talk about it, it's OK. It's just that some of the things you've said add up, and I was just offering my version of the total. Feel free to ignore me if you want to.'

I stared ahead at the maze of lights that seemed to be suspended from the night sky. There was the faint outline of a shore. That was comfort enough. Who needed heart-searching and agony-aunt roles? Not me! All I wanted was for the boat to stop rocking and rolling and to feel solid ground under my feet again.

'I guess you're right,' Mike said quietly. He leaned on the rail next to me, his eyes focused on some imaginary spot in the middle distance. 'Patrick's my hero. Correction. He *was* my hero. Just like Dad, really. And I've modelled myself on him, on them. But Patrick's making it. He'll be a surgeon in the Navy. I'll be a second-rate doctor in some hick town. I'm fairly certain I want to do medicine, but I'm not good enough to be like Patrick. He and Dad, they can do anything. Patrick's a track champion, got into the best frat. house, really good-looking, scared of nothing, and I'm . . .'

'What?' I asked. 'What's wrong with you? You look like an athlete – I saw the way you picked Bel up. It was so expert, and so effortless, that I thought you fancied her! You're good-looking – no, don't argue with me, because it's embarrassing enough for me to say it in the first place – and you're funny, and gentle. You'd make a great children's doctor.'

'A paediatrician? I never thought of that! Yeah. Right. I like working with kids. I helped out at this baseball camp one summer. That was great . . . I only saw as far as surgery, but there's other things as well . . .'

'You don't have to be Patrick. You could be Mike. Like, I could be Megan,' I decided.

'What d'you mean?' he asked.

'Bel. I've always wanted to be Bel. She's wacky and stunning. She never does any work, but I know she'll get better GCSE results than me. She's got a warm, close family, where my parents are a bit weird. And guys just fall over themselves to get at her. She's got style. She goes her own way, and I shuffle along after her, and it's got to stop. If I start being me, I won't have to be jealous of her. I could dye my hair blonde. I could take up tap-dancing – I used to be a pretty fair dancer when I was a kid . . .'

'I could start playing the guitar again. I don't need to follow Patrick around to athletics meets and have him beat me every time . . .' Mike mused.

We were both closed in our own time capsules, talking not really to each other but to the sea and the sky and the lights on the shoreline.

'. . . maybe I can even forget Sandie,' Mike muttered.

'Sandie?'

'A girl in my high-school class. She came with us to Ireland last year. That's why I didn't want to come back,' Mike said. 'We visited distant cousins. She had relatives, too, in that part of Ireland. But she was my girl. Until last year. It's . . . it's a bit difficult . . .'

'Don't tell me about it if you don't want to,' I said quickly.

'Patrick was out to impress her from the start,' Mike continued, as if I hadn't interrupted. 'He was out to impress everyone, all the girls our cousins introduced us to. They were all over Patrick. He'd pick up one, one night, to make up a foursome, and another the next night. But it was always the same. I'd be left talking to this Naimh or Maire, and he'd be dancing with Sandie. The day after we got back, she told me she was finished with me. She's Patrick's girl, now. And every time I think of Ireland, I think of her, and hate him, because he knew what he was doing. He knew he could have anything he wanted, and what he did was to take something away from me. He didn't even have the guts to tell me himself. He left it to her to tell me. He used to be my hero, that's what really hurts. He used to be my hero.'

There wasn't much I could say. Back at Karen's flat he'd understood about me and Terry. When I'd said about love not being about hurting each other, he'd said, 'It's a contest.' He'd been in competition, too, and lost, as I had. His hand lay beside mine on the rail of the deck. It seemed right for me to squeeze his hand, a kind of warm sisterly gesture that said, 'It's OK,' without the need for words. He squeezed in return, and turned to smile at me. I couldn't stop looking into that smile.

'Have you thought,' I murmured, 'that maybe you haven't done so well this year because you've had other things on your mind? Maybe if you'd got all this off your chest at the time, you wouldn't be in the mess you're in now?'

He shrugged. 'I guess I thought I could get over it in my own way. That's what the trip was all about. I had to get away from him this summer. We'd rented a holiday home in Maine, and he was bringing Sandie along, too. So I begged some money from Mom and came over here, not just to get away from them, but to prove I could organize a trip on my own and survive on my own.'

'An ego trip,' I laughed.

He laughed too. 'Right!' he said.

The laughter should have broken the quiet mood that had settled on us. Instead, it cemented it. There we were, hand in hand, sharing confidences and now even sharing jokes, holding on to each other, my eyes looking into his, his into mine. My heart turned over for him, and went on turning over and over like a clown on a trapeze. I wished it would stop. I didn't want to make another mistake.

'I thought, maybe I'll decide to give up on trying to be a doctor. But I'd thought one thing out for sure. I was never, never going back to Ireland,' he murmured.

'If you'd told me all this before, I wouldn't have . . .' I began, apologetically.

'It's OK,' he said. His free hand took hold of my free hand. 'It's OK. It's all different, now. Will you help me, huh? It's a beautiful country. I'd like to share what I know of it.'

'I'd be happy to share it,' I said, swallowing hard. The clown on the trapeze started performing virtuoso moves, defying gravity, defying logic, defying my own reservations about committing myself to being hurt again.

'Would you?' he whispered.

He unlocked one of his hands from mine and, with his fingertips, moved the blowing strands of hair from my face and tucked them behind my ears.

'I can see your freckles again,' he smiled. 'When you were sick, down there, they disappeared, all two hundred and forty-one of them. That's when I knew you were really sick. Now they're all here again. I've been counting!'

He ran his fingers gently across the bridge of my nose, still smiling. The touch trembled inside me, up and down, making my scalp shiver and my toes tingle.

'I like your freckles. I like your green eyes,' he said, quietly.

'Green for envy, eh?' I laughed, too shy and embarrassed to cope with the way I was feeling.

'No. Green for living things. And that red hair. All that life and fire!' he said, running his fingers through my hair. 'Megan . . .'

He lifted my chin with his hand and pulled me towards him gently, until our lips touched. His cheeks were moist and salty with the sea wind. I tasted the salt on his lips, and couldn't think of a single thing to say.

Chapter Thirteen

I was only half-conscious of the scramble to disembark, Kay's twittering, Ricky's unbelievable middle-of-the-night alertness and keenness to drive. Real life was a distant happening. I sat in the back of the car, circled by Mike's arm, wondering if the pins and needles and the circus inside me would ever settle down and allow me to be normal, lonely and miserable again.

I tried to talk sense into my whirling mind. This feeling was not unusual and all reports I'd heard of it pointed to the fact that it wouldn't last. I'd had intimations of the feeling when I was close to Terry, but this was different, lighter, more complete. There was no element of fear. I felt safe and warm. Yet safe only temporarily. This was what was known as a holiday romance, in the magazines, not to be taken seriously. It was the product of too much sun on your head in the day, and too much moonlight at night. It was a longing for touch, so that you wouldn't feel lonely and frightened. It was just one of those passing things, and if I took it too seriously, read too much into it, depended too much on it, I'd be devastated when it was over.

That was the logic. And then there was the argument that said this could be more than little Pete Hanson, because we were friends with enough similarities of experience and temperament to hold us together even without that kiss.

Eventually, there was a kind of desperate resolution that told me no matter what it was, it felt good, and that there was no point in wondering about whether there was any future in this. I'd been given the present. I fell asleep in Mike's arms while the car raced through the night, smiling happily at this conclusion that wasn't a conclusion at all.

At some point during the long drive to the south, Mike woke me, and we all ate breakfast in a white stucco road-house, a roadside cafe which served us with a piled Irish breakfast: thick bacon, golden eggs, warm soda bread and treacle tea. The service was leisurely, the accents soft, and the countryside outside the window a bright emerald-green.

'It's a soft day,' the waitress murmured to us when we left to walk out into the gentle drizzling rain. It felt soft, soft like warm hands.

I couldn't stay awake. I dozed fitfully through villages and towns and long stretches of grey water in the lap of green hills. Sometimes I woke to catch sight of graffiti on village walls, 'Brits go home', a roadside madonna, the shimmer of distant mountains, bungalows like miniature Dallas ranches built in the shelter of a taller decaying farmhouse. It was all fields and green, rolling, hummocky hills, peace and softness.

Mike woke me, somewhere around midday, and helped me out of the car. Vaguely, I remember thanking Kay and Ricky, swapping addresses with them, and then standing with my haversack, waving at the departing car.

'Where are we?' I asked Mike, rubbing my eyes.

'Tralee. Bus station. We're going to catch the next bus to Dingle. That's where my cousins live. Kay and Ricky are going on to Killarney, but I asked them to drop us off here. We've got half an hour's wait, so let's have some sandwiches,' he smiled.

He prepared the sandwiches from the food we'd bought in Carlisle. The butter was melting, rapidly, the cheese was sticky with heat, and the ham beginning to smell, but we ate the sandwiches, sitting side by side on the wall, watching the green buses trundle in and out. I was still dazed, confused by the strangeness of the surroundings and the strangeness of my emotions. I kept glancing at Mike out of the corner of my eye, amazed that he was there, sitting next to me, comfortable with me, thinking of me as life and fire.

He seemed dazed, too. Sometimes he'd smile at me, a relaxed easy smile. Sometimes he squeezed my hand or touched my hair. When the bus for Dingle arrived, he threw away the rest of the rancid butter, the stale bread, decaying cheese and ham, and refastened his haversack very carefully.

'Thanks,' he said, pretending to concentrate on the fastening, not really looking at me.

'For what?' I asked.

'For last night, this morning. For helping me out.'

'Uh?'

'Let's get on the bus,' he smiled.

I don't think the time was right for either of us to say things that might be too specific. Instead, we climbed on to the rattling bus, side by side, for yet another journey onwards. I started to wake up. Perhaps it was the jolting of the bus, the laughter from the passengers, the wind blowing through the open windows, the softness of the morning giving way to clear blue skies. Or perhaps it was that the immediate aftermath of the confessions of the previous night had now passed and left just a heightened sense of being alive, and being grateful for it. But, for the first time since we arrived in Ireland, I looked at it, and it took my breath away. Outside Tralee, the bus climbed into mountains and wound round roads carved into the sky. Below us, water gleamed, running in fast streams, springing from rock, spreading into lakes. I'd seen mountains before, brown and craggy, but these were green to the summit and soft-edged. Once through the pass we came down into tiny lanes, hedged with fuchsia, dripping red and purple blossom, the hedges high as the bus.

'I didn't realize fuchsia was a wild flower, not like this. I'd always thought it was something in a hanging basket or a pot,' I breathed.

'It's like this all over the Dingle peninsula,' Mike smiled, but there was no smugness in the smile, just a sharing of the wonder.

I'd never seen anything so beautiful or so rich. It could have been a million miles from the grimy streets of Liverpool instead of hiding just across the sea. And, at the end of the journey, there was the town of Dingle, streets climbing the hill towards the sea, higgledy houses, rounded Irish writing on the shop fronts and the crazy Irish signposts which announced, on arms pointing in every direction, not only the fictional distance to the nearest towns, but the nearest pubs, hotels and churches.

We slung our haversacks on our backs and started to walk up the main street, towards the sea and the cliffs.

'They'll be surprised to see me,' Mike laughed. 'I hope they're in.'

So did I. The climb up the hill, and the unexpected nature of our arrival, reminded me too forcibly of my arrival with Bel in Haverigg, banging at Pete Hanson's door, having to explain about the failure of that particular holiday romance. I shivered.

'You OK?' Mike asked.

'No problem,' I grinned, quoting him.

'My cousins are Sean and Declan. They're about the same age as us. Declan's at university in Cork, and Sean's still at school in Tralee,' he said. 'You'll get on with them.'

'And the girls?' I asked, nervously.

'Not really cousins, just distant relatives, and there're thousands of them. Two of them, Kate and Maire, live next door, then there's Naimh and Aisling and Theresa down the road. Those are the only names I remember . . . Here.'

He turned in to the front of a large flat-fronted house on the edge of the town.

'Let's see, shall we?' he grinned, banging on the green front door.

There was an immediate rustling of the white net curtains at the window, followed by a shout, then more excited whoops and shouts as heavy footsteps approached the front door and it was flung open by a plump, high-cheeked woman with grey hair and laughing eyes.

'Mother of God, it is! Well, would you look at this! It's Michael, all the way from America, and not a word to tell us you were coming!' the woman cried, hugging him so tightly that he was gasping for breath. 'Declan! Sean! Go out to the garage and tell your father we've got Michael, from America, come to see us.'

'Michael!' A red-haired boy, about my age, appeared behind his mother.

'Is it really him?' another called from the top of the stairs, pounding down towards us.

'OK, Aunty Eileen!' Michael panted, pulling away from her grasp and hugging each of his cousins in turn. 'Sean, Declan . . . this is Megan Griffiths, from Liverpool. We met in the Lake District . . . It's a long story . . .'

'Come on with you both. Tell us over a cup of tea, and Sean, go and get your father! Michael, how long are you staying? Declan, Michael can sleep in your room, and would you see our Bridie's room's aired for the young lady. Mother of God, this is a real surprise.'

She was obviously overwhelmed by Michael's sudden appearance, fanning herself with one hand as she led us into the huge sparkling kitchen at the back of the house, talking incessantly. Michael grinned, unable to get a word in edgeways. Then his Uncle Jimmy burst in through the back door with several small children and a dog, the neighbours were called in, and chaos reigned. I couldn't stop smiling. Everyone was so excited, so pleased to see him, throwing questions at him and not even waiting for replies.

'And how's your mother and father?'

'And Patrick?'

'Did you get the lace we sent at Christmas?'

'Your mother said you were spending the summer in England, so why did you decide to come to Ireland?'

'Kate and Naimh went to the beach at Inch. Just wait till they get back!'

'We've got a party tomorrow night, in Tralee. You'll both be able to come?'

'What was your name again?'

The last question was to me, but even I wasn't allowed to speak before the next questioner butted in. We were both swimming in tea, and filled up with cakes, until I thought I was going to burst. After an hour or so, some of the excitement died down. We were sent to our rooms to freshen up while the family prepared dinner. Bridie's room – Bridie was away in Dublin, nursing – was a bright little room right at the top of the house, with a window overlooking the cliffs and the sea. There was a washbasin in the corner. I washed and changed into my jeans, very conscious that I had nothing really suitable to wear at a celebratory family reunion, but they didn't seem the sort of people who would mind. I tied a bright green ribbon into my hair, and my reflection, in the mirror, smiled back at me with an assurance and confidence I couldn't remember having seen before.

'Maybe I'm actually happy!' I whispered to myself, tripping down the stairs towards the living-room. I could hear Mike's voice from there, explaining the story of how we'd met, and about the lift with Kay and Ricky, and the five pounds bet.

'Five pounds! That's nothing!' a girl's voice squealed.

I opened the living-room door. Mike was sitting in the window-seat like an actor, or a guest at a chat-show, delighting the audience of Aunty Eileen, Uncle Jimmy, Sean and Declan, who were seated around him. But what made my smile freeze, and my heart stop beating, was that two of the most beautiful girls I'd ever seen, both with creamy lightly tanned skin and luxuriant masses of chestnut hair, were perched on the window-seat on either side of him. He had an arm round each of them. I stood framed in the doorway while both girls looked me up and down, down and up, under sneering eyebrows.

'Megan!' Mike beamed, untwining himself, standing, stepping towards me. 'I'd like you to meet Kate and Maire.'

'And me,' a little voice said.

There, in the corner, was a girl like a china doll, perfect, with red-gold hair and a pouting mouth.

'And Naimh,' he added, laughing.

And the doll mouth pursed behind his back at me, in a perfect expression of contempt.

Chapter Fourteen

I realized the strain that Mike was under, having to pay attention to me and to the overjoyed reception he'd been given by his relatives. I understood exactly what he must be going through. He did his best, although there was hardly a moment on that first night, or the next day on the beach, when we could be alone, just to remind ourselves of what had happened between us. So at first I didn't blame him at all, and I couldn't blame the warm close-knit family into which he'd brought a stranger. I blamed the girls.

It was the girls who suggested the day at the beach at Inch, and Mike responded with such enthusiasm that I knew it had to be a special place. It was. We scrambled out of cars on the cliffs to miles of unblemished white sand in a perfect huge bay. With palm trees, it would have made a setting for a tropical paradise advertisement. Aunty Eileen had made a huge picnic for us to take; Declan and Sean had brought guitars, and surfboards, and had the family dinghy on the trailer behind the car. The sun blazed down all day from a cloudless sky. It should have been perfect. But it was different. I felt like an intruder, and the girls, Naimh in particular, did their best to see that I was. Whenever Mike came to sit next to me, to hold my hand, to talk quietly, one of them settled by his side, asking him about his family, reminding him of the times he'd spent there the year before, and, finally, coming up with the question I'd dreaded.

'Where's Sandie?'

Mike handled it very well. He squeezed my hand tightly, but privately, and this was the only indication he gave that the question was difficult for him to cope with.

'She's with Patrick, and my parents, on vacation in Maine,' he smiled.

'With Patrick?' Naimh whistled.

'It was on the cards,' Kate said, sounding not in the least surprised. 'She was the type of girl who went for the obvious.'

'Mmm. I remember going to that disco in Tralee with him, and she spent all night making cow eyes at him. It was just as well you were there, Michael,' Maire cooed.

'Michael was always the nice-natured one,' Kate agreed, talking about him as if he wasn't sitting there and blushing to his toenails.

'I never liked Patrick much, myself,' Naimh said. 'I always had a soft spot for you, Michael.'

Michael squirmed under the adulation at first, but slowly, as the day eased on, or tensed up, depending on how one looked at it, he relaxed into the role of visiting American cheesecake, demonstrated his surfing skills, played a mean game of beach soccer, swam out for miles in the bay with the girls trailing behind him like porpoises, and, at Naimh's request, played the guitar.

He was really very good. Despite my building resentment and my sense that I'd been here before, in the cellar bar with Terry and Bel, always the outsider, Mike drew me back into the charmed and closing circle by singing to me, for me, making it obvious that there was something between us that no amount of beach-bum acting was going to destroy. He started to sing quietly, gently, an old Beatles song, 'Here, There and Everywhere', until Naimh suddenly shouted, 'Let's do "The Irish Rover".'

Declan produced a tin whistle, the girls drummed on their bags and rattled spoons and sang. I joined in with the laughter, too, but the wildness of Irish folk songs had destroyed the private moment.

'Hey, you'll have to come on stage with us tonight, Michael. It'll be a great gas! At the party, our showband's playing. We could fit in an extra guitar,' Declan enthused.

'And a decent vocalist,' Sean muttered, dryly.

'Yeah, Mike, why don't you?' Naimh murmured, snuggling up a little closer to him.

'I don't know,' he considered, looking at me. I nodded. It wouldn't do him any harm to cash in on his talent, to give himself some confidence in the person he could be, once he was out of his brother's shadow.

'It'll mean setting out earlier, and squashing you into the band's van,' Declan said.

'What about Megan?' Mike asked.

'Don't tell us *she* plays the trombone!' Naimh screeched sarcastically.

'It's just that . . .' Mike stammered.

'You can give Megan a lift to the party, can't you, girls?' Sean asked, turning to me, concernedly. 'It's just that we can't really fit two extra bodies in the van, Megan, and we'll have to leave early to set the amps up and do a bit of rehearsing.'

'A *lot* of rehearsing!' Kate giggled. 'Judging from the last time you played together.'

'I'm not sure . . .' Mike said.

'Oh, it'll be OK. What time are you leaving, girls?' Declan asked.

'Seven,' Maire said.

'But we're meeting for a drink at the hotel first,' Naimh said, hurriedly.

'OK. Megan can meet you there, too. At seven?' Declan said.

'Make it half-past,' Naimh said. 'We'll leave the hotel at half-past.'

'So, there you are, Mike. Megan's all fixed up with a lift, and we're fixed up with another guitarist and vocalist. Couldn't be neater,' Declan pronounced.

But I wasn't so sure. Mike seemed happy enough, settled by Declan's obvious assurance. I just didn't like the way Naimh looked at the other two. She was making it very clear that, as far as she was concerned, I was pushing in on something that had started last summer and needed to be finished off.

When we returned from the beach, the misgivings were stronger than ever. Mike had fitted into a familiar enough role, but there wasn't a place for me, except the one he was trying to make. It was almost impossible to speak to him alone about the way I felt. There was a huge meal waiting for us when we returned, a family occasion, another celebration, with everyone talking at once and no room for more than a sidelong glance or two between Mike and me.

I managed to catch up with Mike on the landing between his room and the bathroom while he was racing round to change. He pulled me into his arms for a hurried kiss.

'Isn't this fantastic!' he asked, his eyes bright with enthusiasm. 'It was never like this when I was with Patrick. He just took over. But they're giving me the same sort of welcome – and they want me to play guitar, tonight. I can't believe it! All this, and you as well. But you made it happen. I'd never have come back on my own, with the memories I had.'

'Mike,' I whispered. 'Listen, I don't want to spoil anything for you, but I'm not too happy about the girls. Naimh, in particular. She seems to feel very possessive over you.'

'Over me?' he laughed. 'No, Megan. You've got it all wrong. It's Patrick she's crazy about. He gave her a bad time, last year. I'm just the kid brother. Nothing special.'

'Oh?' I asked.

'Forget her. She doesn't matter. OK, so she's been acting like a dork today, but you'll see, she'll've settled down by tonight. Don't let her worry you.'

'She does,' I admitted. 'She makes me feel as if I'm in the way.'

'Forget it. No problem,' he said, off-handed in his happiness. 'We'll sort it out. Now, I've really got to change. I'll see you later, huh?'

'OK,' I smiled, an uncertain smile. There was no point in pursuing the conversation, but I knew. Perhaps Mike thought he had some experience of jealousy, feeling as he did about Patrick. But jealousy between men is very different from female jealousy. I knew all about it. I knew how I'd felt about Bel, sometimes. Pure spite. And I could read that in Naimh's eyes, too.

Still, I changed, and tried to look good. It was practically impossible. There was nothing even remotely partyish in my haversack, just some creased shorts, a pair of grubby black cotton trousers, and some T-shirts. I longed for some of Bel's rainbow wardrobe so that I could stun the opposition, but I had to settle for the cotton trousers and a white T-shirt with baked-bean stains on the front. I felt dreadful. The effort of the last six days had caught up with me, the emotional upheavals and the struggles to stay cheerful. I threw myself on to Bridie's neat little bed, wrapped myself in the patchwork quilt, and closed my eyes.

Somewhere, distantly, I heard Mike calling that he was leaving. I called back, 'See you later,' but he didn't come up to kiss me goodbye. I curled up into a tight knot, holding on to the pillow, and was woken by Aunty Eileen shouting.

'It's almost half-past seven, Megan. We're going out, now, to the club. The key's in the outhouse if you get back before us!'

Half-past seven! I struggled up, pulled a comb through my tangled curls, wiped the sleep from my eyes and raced downstairs and out, banging the front door behind me.

The hotel was a little way down the main street. It heaved and pulsed with the beat of commercial Irish music. I pushed my way in, past crowds of elderly men in the hallway, into the packed bar which seemed to be taken over by wild pensioners dancing and singing.

'Have you seen Naimh and Kate and Maire?' I asked the girl behind the bar.

She shook her head slowly.

'I seen them,' a girl interrupted. She was standing by the bar, balancing a glass of wine over the heads of stampeding elderly ladies. 'They left almost half an hour ago, before this lot came in. Said they were going to a party in Tralee and couldn't wait. Are you something to do with the American?'

I nodded.

'I heard them saying they were supposed to meet you here. Well, Kate said that, but Naimh was keen to get away, if you know what I mean? I think she fancies her chances with . . . Mike . . . is that his name?'

Again, I nodded, swallowed hard, and asked, 'So what time did they leave?'

'Seven . . . seven-fifteen, some time around there,' the girl said.

I squeezed down into the only free seat in the bar. I had to sit. Around me the women started singing 'Rose of Tralee'. Two huge tears squeezed out of my eyes and fell on the sticky table.

'Awr eh!' the woman sitting next to me complained, nudging me in the ribs. 'This is a good one. It's not a weepie.'

There was a familiarity about her accent that didn't strike me for a moment. I was too deep into my own private misery. I heard her voice as Irish. But it wasn't.

'You're Scouse!' I sniffed.

'Bootle,' she said proudly. 'Alice, we've just found a little Liverpool girl. Look! Here!'

Alice, her huge friend, peered round at me through pebble glasses and the Guinness she was drinking.

'Welcome home,' she said, raising her glass to me. 'Nice to meet you, love. What're you doing here?'

'I'm lost,' I sobbed. 'I just got stood up by some mates of my boyfriend.'

'That doesn't make sense,' the first woman said.

'It makes Irish sense,' Alice decided.

'What're you doing here?' I asked, in return.

'Oh, it's not just us two, love. Not just me and Ivy. There's a coach-load of us. We've been touring Ireland all week, one of those St Patrick Tours, and we're on the way back on the coach . . . Didn't you see it outside?'

'The leprechauns must've taken it,' Ivy said,

breaking off from the chorus of 'When Irish Eyes Are Smiling'.

'The leprechauns must've been at my purse, too, Ivy. I'm running out of that funny Irish money,' Alice complained.

'Three small Guinness over here, Jack!' Ivy called to a round bald man who was standing at the bar. 'You'll join us, won't you?' she asked.

It was my first glass of Guinness. It wasn't my last. I sat with the two pensioners, joined in the singing, and told my story very sadly. Ivy and Alice sniffed.

'I never trusted Americans,' Alice said.

'Not since the war, and that Chuck from Cincinnati,' Ivy nodded wisely.

'They give you chewing gum and nylons, and then it's "Ta-ta, I'm off".'

'It wasn't him. It wasn't him. It's those girls,' I tried to explain, thickly.

'It always is. It's always The Other Woman,' Alice slurred.

'I want to go home,' I decided.

'Well . . .' Alice said.

'Well?' Ivy twinkled. 'Jack!' she shouted. 'Is there room for one more under the seats? This kid's got no money and a broken heart, and she's from Croxteth.'

'One under the seat wouldn't hurt. She can look after the empties.'

'Can I?' I asked, dazedly.

'Why not?' Alice asked. 'Where's your luggage?'

'I'll go and get it, shall I?'

'We'll wait,' Ivy smiled, sipping at yet another Guinness. 'We're in no hurry.'

'Not until closing time. We'll be leaving at closing time,' Alice said.

I lurched up, out of the hotel, and along the main

street to the O'Connor house. It took me a while to find the key in the outhouse. It took me even longer to write the note to Michael, telling him that I was on my way back to Liverpool. My head wasn't very clear, so my reasons for leaving weren't very clear, either. I was just overwhelmed with the feeling that I wasn't wanted, and somehow I tied him in with that sense of rejection, of having been left in a strange town by three witches out for my blood and an American scalp. I collected my haversack, stuffed all my clothes into it, found the remaining three pounds twenty of our original stake money, and left the house, holding the money tightly in my hand. It just might pay for two glasses of Guinness – the price of my fare back to Liverpool.

Chapter Fifteen

I was crazy – crazy mad, crazy angry, and crazy to believe that looking at life through the bottom of an empty glass of Guinness could give anything but a distorted view of the way things really stood. But the craziness was sufficient to make me an illegal passenger on a bus heading for Dublin and, by way of another boat-trip, for Liverpool and home.

Perhaps the craziness was as much to do with the company as with the Guinness. I'd felt an alien. Alice and Ivy and the other thirty or so teenaged pensioners had reminded me of what it felt like to have total acceptance without striving for understanding first. To them, I was just a kid from home, and home was a very special place, distinguished from the rest of the world by an impenetrable accent and a fiercely chauvinistic loyalty. The age-gap didn't matter. I cried. They cried. They sang. I joined in. The bus journey through the night was a non-stop party with crates in the aisle, frequent roadside stops for nausea and toilets, and a running cabaret. Jack did his Bing Crosby impressions, a petite blue-rinsed woman called Brigit did a raucous interpretation of 'My Way' before passing out, and the high spot of the night, repeated almost hourly, was the full choral version of 'You'll Never Walk Alone' with arm-in-arm swaying in formation through the flat plains of central

Ireland. Eventually, on the outskirts of Dublin, most of the group fell asleep, snoring happily. I did, too, snuggled between Alice and Ivy on the back seat, without a care in the world. At least, that's the way I felt.

The enormity of the cares only began to trickle through to my deadened brain when I awoke as the coach eased forward, and Alice and Ivy gently pushed me to the floor and threw their coats on to me. I crouched under the fake fur and the yellow plastic mac for what seemed like hours, although it can't have been more than half an hour or so. Lying in cigarette ash, attacked by the occasional rolling bottle, I began to add up the consequences of a glass of Guinness.

For a start, I was an illegal extra on that bus, and I would be on the boat. Despite the collusion of the bus driver and the gangster pensioners, I was having to hide out, and would have to make myself as unnoticeable as possible on the boat. Alice and Ivy whispered instructions to me, plotted and schemed. It was all part of their holiday, just another laugh. But it was beginning to worry me. The two of them managed, once the bus had settled in its place in the hold of the ferry, to smuggle me out past the eyes of the ticket inspectors and ferry crew, but would they be able to smuggle me back on to the bus? They assured me that they would when they found me a seat on deck.

'Just don't say nuthin',' Ivy instructed me, wrapping me in her fake fur.

'Pretend to be foreign or daft. That's the best idea. If anyone talks to you,' Alice added. 'We'll bring you something to eat, later on, if I win on the Bingo we're organizing. We'll be in Liverpool by four o'clock!'

'Four o'clock!' I howled. I'd expected the boat-trip to be as short as the one from Stranraer.

'Great, isn't it? I don't mind foreign countries, but it's nice to get home,' she said, patting my head. 'See you later, love.'

So I was stuck on deck for what would be hours, with nothing to do but brood on the rest of my worries. Like the fact that I had only an Irish tenpence piece in my pocket, and an empty, hung-over stomach. No legal status, no money . . . and no love.

That last feeling came on me slowly as the boat ploughed through the grey sea. No love. I remembered standing, leaning over the railing in the night on the other ferry, sick to the pit of my stomach, and yet slowly, beautifully, falling in love with a boy who wasn't quite sure who he was, and whose uncertainty was something I could identify with, and reach out to. That Stranraer ferry had brought me something I'd needed. I'd discovered that love isn't so much a feeling as something you do – offering help, talking, stepping out together into the unknown. Mike had stepped unexpectedly into my life. I'd loved him, and I'd stepped out, and the gap he left was as deep and grey as the sea we ploughed across, now.

I sat numb with cold, hunched tightly, thinking, cursing my stupidity and the insecurity that had made me leave. It really wasn't his fault. It wasn't Naimh's. It was mine. In my heart I was still the reject I believed myself to be, setting other people's teeth on edge, getting only what I deserved.

Alice and Ivy brought a ham sandwich and a cardboard mug of tea up to me at about two o'clock, shivered on deck, and left again for the smoky comfort of another Bingo game. I watched seagulls and saw the shoreline approach, as grey as the sea, through the blur of tears. No one spoke to me. No one noticed me. At a little before four, the conspirators returned again, dragging me from the dismal view of mud-flats, power-stations and industrial wastelands, and pushed me into the middle of the milling crowd of pensioners queuing to get back on to the bus. I crept in, hidden behind Alice's bulk and Ivy's coat, took up my position on the floor of the bus and had never felt so desolate before.

I knew how I should be feeling: confident, victorious, smug, very pleased with myself. A part of me felt those things. I'd been away from home for seven days, and in those seven days I'd changed, inside, beyond all recognition. But no one would know. The bleakness of having lost what I'd been looking for would make everyone believe that I was the same Megan Griffiths who had left home a lifetime ago.

I felt the bus jolt up the ramp and drive on to solid ground. A cheer deafened me. Ivy pulled her coat from me.

'You can come up now, love. We're back!'

Jack started singing, tiredly at first, but gaining heart as the Liver Buildings swung into view. It was 'You'll Never Walk Alone' again. I linked arms with Ivy and Alice and joined in, croakily, remembering all that walking, remembering the bread van, the old couple who'd taken us to Windermere, the ferret and his gorilla friend, Nick and Jess, Karen, Kay and Ricky, Bel and . . . and Mike. I hadn't really been alone until now.

'Where d'you want dropping off? We're going back to Bootle,' the driver called back to me.

'Here. This'll do!' I yelled.

We were at the Pier Head. It was as good a place as anywhere. Alice and Ivy helped me off. The pensioners waved, shouted and cheered. I thanked them all, hugged Ivy and Alice, little fat Jack and the bus driver. Someone shoved a bottle of Guinness into my hand and then the bus roared off, leaving me standing with my haversack, dressed still in the T-shirt with the baked-beans stain and my grubby black trousers, in the Liverpool rain, at the Pier Head, in the rush-hour, with only an Irish ten-pence piece to my name.

I found a telephone box that hadn't been vandalized, eventually, and phoned home.

'Mum, it's me. I'm at the Pier Head. Can you come and meet me?' I asked, wearily.

'Megan? Megan, is that you?' she squealed. 'Are you on your own?'

'Yes. It's me, Mum,' I repeated, surprised by the warmth in her voice. 'Alone.'

'Oh, thank God! Bel came back days ago, giving us some garbled story about how you'd gone on to Scotland with an American student you'd met, and, well . . . you can't be too sure of strangers, these days. We've been worried sick, even your dad . . . Bill! Bill! Megan's back! She's at the Pier Head, of all places. No, I'll go. All right, all right, we'll *both* go. Stay there, Megan. No. Go and stand by the entrance to the Albert Dock. We'll pick you up there. Your dad's insisting on coming along, too. We won't be more than ten minutes!'

Her happiness verged on the hysterical. And for Dad to turn out to pick me up from anywhere was a once-in-a-blue-moon occurrence. I pulled a surprised face at the telephone receiver before putting it back on its rest and walking back to the Albert Dock. I sat on my haversack, waiting, feeling just a little more heroic and a thousand times more loved and needed than I had just an hour or so ago.

I'd go to see Bel as soon as I arrived home. No, I wouldn't. I'd have a bath. Then I'd change. Then I'd walk into them all in the cellar. Bel would fall off her chair in amazement. I'd produce a postcard I'd bought in Dingle to prove that I'd been to Ireland, and the stub from my Stranraer to Larne passenger ticket that Kay had bought for me. I'd be very enigmatic about Mike. That would be one in the eye for Terry, and I'd try to drop hints to Bel that I'd had to tear myself away from Mike's desperate embraces to come back home, and that I'd left him heartbroken. I could, perhaps, suggest that he'd begged me to write to him, but that I'd refused because I'd never really fancied him. I could be terribly off-hand and dismissive about Americans, generally. That would go down a bomb with Terry. I could get away with this one. I'd been hiding my feelings successfully for months. One deception more wasn't going to hurt anyone but me, and could convince everyone but me that I could live a lie and a heartbreak.

A frantic tooting on a car-horn woke me from my plans for a future as a double agent. I looked up to see Mum stumbling towards me, her arms wide.

'Megan!' she shouted, as I fell into her hug. She cried all over my limp greasy hair. I cried a little, too, quite overwhelmed by the sudden display of affection. 'We've missed you!' she said. 'You look wonderful. Tanned, too! Who would've believed it? And older. Much older. What happened? Oh, and your exam results arrived. They're very good. Your dad says . . . Oh, we'd better get back to the car. I forgot he was there!' she laughed through her tears as the tooting started again.

Dad nodded when we ran up and fell through the open doors of the car. His eyes were shiny.

'Well, young lady,' he said. 'Well . . .'

'All the way to Scotland!' Mum said, proudly, fastening her seat-belt.

'Ireland, too,' I said.

Dad had been pulling out into the traffic. The car lurched and stalled.

'Ireland?' he gulped.

'West coast. This American had relatives there. We got a lift with some other Americans in Scotland, who just happened to be doing the Stranraer to Larne crossing, so that's where we ended up.'

Dad shook his head and made another attempt to find a place in the stream of rush-hour traffic.

'Ireland . . .' he murmured, obviously very impressed. 'We've never been to Ireland.'

'It's beautiful!' I enthused. 'You wouldn't believe it. There's big hedges that're all fuchsia, and we went to a beach just like something out of paradise and . . .'

I rattled on and on, all the way home. Dad gaped, Mum kept looking at me as if I were an impressive visiting lecturer.

'What now?' Mum asked, when we arrived.

'Oh . . . a bath. Then a little rest. Food, if you've got any. And I thought I'd just go down to the cellar place tonight, you know, to see if Bel's there,' I said off-handedly, wandering in through the kitchen, examining the living-room, peering up the stairs. It was still the same. Nothing had altered. Except perhaps the way Mum and Dad were treating me. Except perhaps the way I felt.

'I might just have a rest *before* my bath,' I yawned.

I climbed up to my bedroom, threw my haversack on the chair, crawled fully clothed under my duvet, and fell asleep, dreaming of paradise and fuchsia and a smile I'd never see again.

Chapter Sixteen

Mum brought me breakfast in bed at nine o'clock the next morning. I was still in my T-shirt, still rolled in the duvet. I'd slept for sixteen hours, the exhaustion of the last week finally catching up with me.

'Bel phoned just now, so I thought I'd better wake you,' she smiled, hotching me up in bed and setting a heaped tray in front of me. 'She says they're coming round at ten. She's bringing that boyfriend of hers.' Mum wrinkled her nose and pursed her mouth. Terry wasn't one of her favourite characters. 'Something about taking you out for the day to Southport. Apparently, you won your bet.'

'Great,' I said, trying to sound enthusiastic. I wasn't. A week ago, a trip to Southport with Terry would have been the stuff that dreams were made of. Now, it all seemed a waste of time. And effort.

I had barely an hour to polish up my act. I practised various approaches while I devoured the poached eggs, mushrooms and toast that Mum had made for me.

'Well, naturally, there was no point in getting really involved with someone who lives thousands of miles away,' I heard myself saying inside my head. 'So I thought I'd break it off before it got too heavy.' Or I could try the pseudo-honest approach: 'We were just friends.'

Or perhaps, 'You know me, Terry, the original frozen carrot. That's all there was to it.'

Mum came back into my bedroom, just as I was getting a little blur-eyed over that one.

'I've run a bath for you,' she murmured. 'And here. If you're going to Southport, you'll need this.' She handed me two ten-pound notes. 'It's the money we saved from not having you around for a week. Enjoy yourself, eh. And, Meg . . .'

'Mmm,' I said, trying to hide behind my mug of tea.

'About this American student . . . What happened? Last night you were garbling about how you had to stow away on the ferry with a group of pensioners. It all seemed a bit sudden. So, why . . .? Did this boy . . .?'

'No, Mum,' I said, trying to laugh, trying to practise out loud the lies I'd been practising in silence. 'No funny business. It wasn't anything like that. It was just, you know . . .'

I couldn't make any of the lies work.

'. . . I was in the way. I liked him. A lot. I thought he liked me. But there were some other girls, in Ireland, with other ideas. I . . . Oh, it doesn't matter,' I gulped, wiping my eyes on the sheet, jumping out of bed.

'Meg!' Mum called after me as I raced to the bathroom, but I didn't look round. I couldn't. I locked myself in the bathroom, took one look at my tear-stained grubby face, my hair still matted from the sea wind, and leapt into the bath to try to wash the memories away. Over and over again I dunked my head under the water, dousing it with shampoo, scrubbing at it viciously. But Mike was still there, holding my face in his cupped hands, whispering about fire and life and love. I couldn't bear it. It was far worse than the pathetic dreams I'd had about Terry. They were only dreams. This was too real, too raw. How could I pretend it had never happened, and how could I have run away from it? Now, I had to get on with living with it.

I towelled my hair dry, viciously, cleaned my teeth, pampered my shiny skin with some body cream, and shuffled into my bedroom. Today, I really was going to try to start living with it. I chose a dress from the rail in my wardrobe, a pale green cotton with a scoop neckline and a plunging back, to show off the glow that a week's trekking through sunshine had given me. I pinned my still-damp hair into a crown of curls with emerald combs, and slid my aching feet into strappy sandals. If I couldn't feel good, at least I could look good. I smiled at myself, experimentally, in my bedroom mirror. My eyes didn't smile back. They were still misted, like a cloudy mirror.

There was a knock on the front door. This was it. Bel and Terry. 'Hello, young lovers! Yes, don't I look great! Just performed a little DIY bypass surgery on my bleeding heart, and now everything's just wonderful!'

'I'll get it!' I shouted, racing down the stairs, fire and life in motion, radiant, smiling, the best performance of my miserable life. At least I had other things to see me through. I'd found a little confidence from somewhere. I'd learned about self-sufficiency, and sleeping in a bender. I'd handled money with ruthless efficiency. I'd fought off a ferret. And someone had kissed me and meant it. Someone had loved me. Someone . . .

'Hi, Bel!' I beamed, flinging the door open.

'Hi,' Mike said.

He was just there, standing on the doorstep,

holding his address book in a trembling hand, holding his rucksack in the other. A taxi was pulling away from the kerb.

'I . . . er . . . had your address . . . remember? I . . . thought . . . I thought I'd like to have a look at Liverpool before I went home . . . No . . . I thought . . . Look, I'm here. I wanted to see you again. Do you mind?'

'Mike!' I sobbed, launching myself into his arms. He dropped his haversack on to the step and held me tightly, pressing his face against my damp hair.

'Naimh's car broke down on the way to the party. They didn't arrive until eleven. I was going out of my mind panicking about you, and then you weren't there . . . I think I shook her. Declan had to pull me away. Kate told me how they'd left you behind, then I got back, and found your note . . . I knew how you felt. But I couldn't just let you go. I couldn't . . .' he cried.

'Megan!' my mum called from the kitchen. 'Megan, who's there? Megan – Bel, Terry and Benno just arrived at the back door. Are you coming through?'

'Come on. Come on in,' I whispered to Mike.

We pulled the haversack into the hall and left it there while we walked hand in tight hand towards the others. Mike wiped the tears from my cheeks before I pushed the kitchen door open.

Terry Macdolan was standing, leaning up against the fridge, his arm round Bel, supreme defeated arrogance in his wicked gap-toothed grin. He was doing his best to try to show me that I'd lost, even if I thought I'd won. His mouth was ready to shape round some snide put-down. And even the grin did nothing for me. He was just someone I'd known a long time ago, standing there with a grin falling off the edges of his mouth.

But, as I looked at the slipping smile, and the

drooping shoulders, I realized that even without Mike at my side I was a match for Terry, now. He didn't scare me at all. He hadn't travelled four countries on a fiver. He was just an armchair cynic, not someone who put his insecurities on the line.

'Bel, Terry,' I nodded to them both, knowing who and what I was at last, no vague feelings, just certainties. 'Mum . . . this is Michael O'Connor. I think he'd like to stay for a while.'

THE END